THE
Sanctuary

The Sanctuary: Romance, Murder & Mystery
Copyright © 2024 by Joanne 'Gram' Radke & Shirley K. Smith

Published in the United States of America

Library of Congress Control Number: 2024911817
ISBN   Paperback: 979-8-89091-767-6
ISBN   Hardback: 979-8-90000-027-5
ISBN   eBook: 979-8-89091-768-3

All rights reserved. No part of this publication may be reproduced, stored in a retrieval system or transmitted in any way by any means, electronic, mechanical, photocopy, recording or otherwise without the prior permission of the author except as provided by USA copyright law.

The opinions expressed by the author are not necessarily those of ReadersMagnet, LLC.

ReadersMagnet, LLC
10620 Treena Street, Suite 230 | San Diego, California, 92131 USA
1.619. 354. 2643 | www.readersmagnet.com

Book design copyright © 2024 by ReadersMagnet, LLC. All rights reserved.

Cover design by Jhiee Oraiz
Interior design by Daniel Lopez

JOANNE 'GRAM' RADKE & SHIRLEY K. SMITH

THE SANCTUARY

ROMANCE, MURDER & MYSTERY

DEDICATION

I dedicate this book to my dear friend and co-author Shirley K. Smith, who has been a dear friend and mentor to me for so many years. "It was a joy to co-write this with you and to finally get our creation into print. I am so looking forward to seeing you once again on the other side where you have resided for the past twelve years."

I would also like to dedicate this book to Shirley's family, as she would want to do, if she was able. "You have all been such a blessing. Thank you. Until we meet again, on the other side!"

Kirby & Shelly Smith,

Kelly Anne Smith,

Nicole & Lorne Pike, Jacob and Hannah,

Craig & Helena Smith, Gloria and Liam

THANK YOU

I would like to thank you, my reader, for picking this book up to read and expand your imagination. I pray that this will entertain you and give you another exciting adventure to enjoy as much as we enjoyed creating it for you.

We only ask that you read it and pass it on to another when you are finished with it… and please don't forget to write a review of your thoughts and comments when you are done.

Go to Amazon.com or Amazon.ca type in The Sanctuary or Joanne Radke and write a review in the book section. Thank you!

IN THE BEGINNING...

Janice Rogers and Sharon Stevenson stood on the snow-covered lawn of the old mansion with hearts full of joy and anticipation. They had stood on this very spot and prayed for this day to come when they were only ten years old. It took over forty years, but God heard their prayer, and now He was answering them in a beautiful way.

"Oh, Janice, we can develop this property into the Retreat Center we've always dreamed about. It is a home away from home with great food and beautiful, serene surroundings. A place to be refreshed and enjoy God's beauty! It doesn't look so great right now, but with paint, landscaping, and a lot of elbow grease, it will be perfect."

"Yeah, just think, after all these years, we are back together and are seeing our dream come true. It's awesome! God is so good! We have three months until opening. We can do this!

With Lawrence Mackay's handy work, your decorating skills, and my love of fixing things, we'll get it ready in plenty of time," exclaimed Janice.

The old Victorian mansion needed repairs, but not so many that it would take months and months to complete. The house was originally quite magnificent, and they knew they could bring it back to its elegant self and make it even better with all the modern conveniences.

Sharon and Janice went into the house to check out the small apartment located on the top floor of the three-story house. As they went into the apartment, Janice squealed as a mouse ran by, "Oh no, I never thought of mice! I hate mice!"

Sharon laughed. "Oh, Janice, what did you expect? This house has been unoccupied for ages. Let's hope that's all that's inhabiting this old relic!

This will work perfectly for us. With two large bedrooms, we can each have a place to chill out after a long day with our guests."

"It'll be great, but let's get rid of these mice, the first thing on our list of things to do,'" exclaimed Janice.

They wandered through the house, making a list of all the things that needed to be done. "Definitely needs painting in every room, modern equipment in the kitchen, bathrooms updated, a new furnace, and lots of little repairs." Upon finishing the tour of the inside, they went and stood on the soon-to-be-be-beautiful wrap-around porch. "We probably need a new roof as well."

Sharon felt a chill in the air. "I'll be glad when it warms up. Can't you imagine sitting out here on a warm summer night? White wicker furniture and tall glasses of lemonade. Listening to the loons on the lake. I can't wait to see this all finished. It will be so beautiful!"

"Well, let's get to work and start making this dream come true!"

Janice had been a missionary in Africa for many years, and Sharon had raised a wonderful family and was a widow for just five years. They both suffered tragedy in their lives, and the dark times brought them back together. They were a great support to each other, and it seemed like they had never been apart. Both were financially stable, so they could invest to make this gem a true sanctuary with no financial worries.

Sharon had a son, Daniel, who was in the travel business and through him they were able to get guests booked early now, before they would open. He had used the architect's sketch to entice visitors, and all six rooms with his mother's descriptions had already been taken.

Sharon had each room all planned out and named even before the built out and renovation.

Janice's cell phone rang. "Hello, Janice Rogers here!"

"Janice, it's Lawrence Mackay. I have some bad news. I'm so sorry, but my daughter has been in a terrible car accident.

My wife and I must go to Toronto to help with the kids. It looks very bad, and I don't know how long we'll be away. I'm so sorry, but you're going to have to get someone else to help with the renovations."

"Oh, Lawrence, I'm so sorry. How is she doing? We will pray for her. Do you know of anyone else we can get in town to help us out?"

"No, perhaps you could put an ad in our local paper? I don't know of anyone who would be available for the time you need. I'm so sorry!" exclaimed Lawrence.

"Oh, that's okay! You have enough to worry about. Let us know how your daughter is doing alright? Thank you, and bye for now!"

Janice ended the call and commented her disappointment to Sharon, "Well, there goes our carpenter-handyman. He suggested we put an ad in the local paper. I know it doesn't have a large circulation, but we'll pray and need to put our trust in the Lord!"

"That's what we'll have to do, Janice. So, let's write up an ad now and take it into town. The sooner we do, the better."

That afternoon, as Janice and Sharon drove into town, they couldn't help but notice how quiet it was this time of year. The tall, stately pine trees were still covered with snow, and they made it look like a winter wonderland. The banks of snow along the road now looked grey from the clearing of the roads. It certainly didn't look like the bustling town of the summer months. Joe's Cafe was still lit up like a Christmas tree. The stores lining both sides of the main street had sale signs in their windows still claiming, 'The Best Bargains in Town!'

The ladies went into The Banner to place their ad. The small newspaper shop smelled of ink and musk. Pops had been running this paper for fifty years and knew every person in town.

Sharon was the first to speak to him. "Hi Pops, how are you doing?"

"Well, let's say I take each day as it comes. Don't get too riled up about things, so I can say I'm doing pretty good. How about you?"

"I'm great. You remember Janice! She was away in Africa."

"Yea, I remember the two of you little scalawags. You used to be pullin' pranks together all the time!" he shared. They all chuckled as they remembered the messes they used to get into.

"I particularly remember the time you let the cows out of Peter Townsend's field; they were all over the road, and it took him hours to round them up!"

They all laughed as Sharon and Janice remembered that incident well. "We both got our backsides paddled and were grounded for a week." Sharon smiled at Janice. "Yeah, and we weren't allowed to speak to each other either for quite a while after that one. It was a good thing that we knew how to text. We kept in touch even though we weren't supposed to 'speak' to each other."

"Pops, we have an ad we need to place in your paper today. We need a handyman, and we need him pronto!"

"You're in luck. I'll type set it up today as the paper comes out tomorrow!" replied Pop.

Janice and Sharon left the shop. Janice's stomach started to growl. "Let's hurry over to Joe's and grab a bite to eat. I'm starving."

Joe's Cafe was a gathering place for the town. He and his wife, Tori, knew everyone and their business.

Not too much got past them. They, like Pops, had lived here a good many years. Tori looked to the door as the ladies walked in from the bitter cold.

"Janice and Sharon, you're a sight for sore eyes. I heard you bought the old Beaverton mansion up on the hill."

"What are you up to?" asked Tori.

Sharon spoke first, "We're going to renovate it and make it a retreat center, a new Bed and Breakfast. You knew we always loved that place. Now it's ours!" Janice sat down and looked at the menu. "What's good today, Tori?"

"You know better than that? Everything we serve is beyond good. It beats all those fast-food places. What would you like?"

"I'll have the Philly steak on a bun with fries. What about you, Sharon?"

"I'll have a Greek salad with Chicken on it." replied Sharon.

"Things don't change much with you two! Bet you'll have dessert with that salad, Sharon," asked Tori.

They all laughed. It was good to be back in their old childhood stomping grounds. So many happy times of long ago.

The place hadn't changed much either through the years. Still, the same aqua paint color on the walls, freshly painted, however. Chrome tables and chairs with cream upholstery. Bar stools at the counter to match the chairs. Even though it looked like it was back in the 50s, it felt like home, and the food was great, too, and the company was so very friendly.

Sharon noticed a very good-looking man eating at the counter.

He seemed to be quite friendly with Joe. I wonder where he came from and what would a hunk like that be doing here?

After the meal, they drove to the Twilight Motel, where they stayed until the apartment in the mansion was ready for them to move into.

Sharon sighed, "I've missed this place more than I can say. One thing I'm surprised at, though, is I thought there would be some mention of the murders that have been happening here?"

"Maybe they like to forget about them. I wonder if it's stopped people from coming here. There certainly has been enough publicity since the Sheriff hasn't been able to solve them yet," commented Janice. "I just pray we are far enough removed from it at The Sanctuary. Let's pray it won't affect our guests or business!"

～～～

Jason Morris had to find a place to fit in while he investigated the strange murders that happened in this small town over the past three years. Staying at this motel wasn't cutting it. He needed to go undercover and fit in with the locals more. "Please, Lord, make a way for me."

Jason bought the local paper the very next day, and there, right before his eyes, was an ad for a live-in handyman. *Wow, God is quick! I need to get The Bureau to make a false resume, giving me all the credentials, I need. I hope they don't screw it up this time. The time I needed one for an undercover job a few months ago just did not work! This is just too important for them to mess it up again!* Jason thought.

Jason drove out to The Sanctuary to have a look to see if this place would fit in with his plans. He drove to the side of the road to the driveway, parked, and walked in through the dense trees to have a look. It was hard walking with the build-up of snow on the walk.

He thought to himself, *why didn't I think to wear boots? My feet are going to be soaked!* There was a car parked in the driveway by the house, so he had to be careful.

It was a beautiful spot, at least what he could see from the trees. It looked like there was a boathouse on the lake. This property would be ideal. It would also give him the opportunity to do all the carpentry projects he loved to do.

He remembered how he used to watch and learn from his dad how to create beautiful pieces of furniture and other things. The woodworking projects he had done in the past would certainly be of benefit to him now. "Please, God, let this be the place!" He prayed.

The next day, early in the morning, Janice and Sharon met with the exterminator. Sharon shook his hand, "Nice to meet you, Mr. Lowen. Can you get rid of these pesky mice quickly?"

"We need to start working, and neither of us like the thought of little feet running up our legs."

"I'll have this done in no time. Have you ever thought of getting yourself a cat? It would keep away any mouse that dares come near you."

"That's not a bad idea. However, some people are allergic to cats, and with the guests, that could be a problem!"

"If you restrict the cat, say, to your apartment, it shouldn't be a problem!" replied Mr. Lowen.

"We'll think on that one, and besides, we have a large dog that will help. I admit they don't go after mice like cats, but most people enjoy a dog!" explained Sharon.

"Sharon, why don't we get a cat for our apartment?" asked Janice.

"That way we won't have to worry about the guests, and it can take care of any future mice situations both in the apartment and in the Sanctuary."

"I guess that would be all right. Once we get this apartment livable, we'll go into town and see if the Humane Society has one that we could adopt."

Jason was on his way to an appointment at The Sanctuary with Janice and Sharon. "I'm asking Lord that you help me with this interview. I don't know why I'm feeling so nervous about this. What's the matter with me?" he prayed.

Jason drove up the long driveway, thinking how beautiful this drive would be in the Spring, Summer, and particularly the Fall. Large maple trees lined either side of the driveway.

Jason imagined what it would be like driving under a large green cathedral of lush foliage.

He drove up to the house and parked his car. The front door opened, and two rather striking beauties walked out to greet him. He recognized them from the Cafe in town when he was having lunch a couple of days ago. This could be very interesting, he thought.

As Jason shook their hands, he was a little startled as he looked into the eyes of the dark-haired, bluer-than-blue eyes of Sharon. Something just clicked! Janice was a looker as well, with touches of red in her hair, and hazel's eyes seemed to change as she moved. She was the shorter of the two. I would guess they're in their fifties and have taken very good care of their physical appearance. I wonder what their spiritual conditions are like, he wondered.

Sharon invited Jason in. "We have looked at your resume, and it appears to be in good order. We have also checked your references.

We'll show you around, and you can ask any questions as we are walking through the property. Okay?"

Jason could see that a little paint, and fixings, making sure everything is up to building code would make this old place a beauty. "When are you planning on opening?"

"April 15th," both chimed in.

"Your ad mentioned you have an apartment that I could live in!"

Janice took the lead. "Yes, it's in the Boathouse. Come along. It's this way."

As they went to the lake, Sharon was feeling a little confused. When she shook hands with Jason, there was a spark that went right through her to the tip of her toes.

She had not felt that kind of a thrill for a long time. What was going on?

The apartment in the Boathouse was not in bad shape. It could use a coat of paint and was quite livable. It would suit Jason perfectly. He could come and go without notice by anyone at the mansion on his off times and keep his commitment to the ladies at The Sanctuary.

"Well, Jason, do you think you could fill this position for us, and if so, when could you start?"

"I could start tomorrow. When could I move into the apartment?"

Both ladies smiled, but Janice spoke up as she looked at Sharon. "Good, you're hired! You can move in right away, but we'll all have to do some cleaning first!"

"No problem, let me look after that. You have enough to do with the house. If you have bedding and some cleaning equipment, I will move in today so I can start first thing in the morning."

"We'll have bedding available for you when you come back with your things." Sharon just remembered the mice in the main house. "You had better check for mice, as we've hired an exterminator to clean them out of the main house."

"I'm not too worried about mice. Just give me some mouse traps and peanut butter, and I'll have them out of here in no time!"

Jason was so excited. Thank you, God. I know this is you. Please help me to do all that I need to do with the investigation and the job here.

He hadn't had time to develop relationships over the years except for one very bad time earlier in his life. As a result, Jason steered away from women and concentrated on his career.

I must admit that something happened with Sharon with that handshake. I'm not sure exactly what, but I need to keep my eyes on the investigation and not on the owner of The Sanctuary, he said to himself.

As time passed by, Janice and Sharon worked on the apartment as Jason worked on the rest of the house. Janice wanted to feel the safety of the cat, so it was full speed ahead with the apartment. It was up to conditions suitable to both Sharon and Janice, and they were now ready to move it.

The first thing the next morning, Sharon and Janice drove into town to see about getting a cat.

"I hope they have a nice cat that we can love and enjoy. I always wanted a cat, but my mom was very allergic to cats.

This would fulfill one of my childhood dreams.

Sharon smiled, "Well, I hope we can make one of your dreams come true!"

On entering the Humane Society doors, they could hear loud barking and meowing. It sounded like a zoo.

Janice approached the counter and said, "Hi, I am Janice Rogers, and this is Sharon Stevenson. We are looking to adopt a cat. Do you have a nice house cat that would catch mice?"

"Hi Janice, my name is Jeff Jones. Why don't we go to the back and see if there is one that you would like?"

As soon as they saw the cats, Janice said, "I love that one."

"It is so beautiful. I love the colours. It reminds me of the book I read as a child about a calico cat. Is it a 'he' or a 'she'?"

"It's neither, it has been neutered. It is a year old and was turned in because the owner died, and there was no one to take it in."

"Then let's do all that we have to do to adopt it. Does it have a name?"

"The owner called it Mr. Tipps, and that is what we call it."

"Mr. Tipps it is then!"

They filled out all the paperwork and Mr. Jones got a carrier and off they went. They stopped by the Hardware store to pick up the supplies they would need to take care of Mr. Tipps.

"Thanks Sharon, for making one of my dreams come true!"

"You are such a delight and so easy to please. Don't forget this is your cat and you are responsible for it!"

There was a lot to be done to get The Sanctuary ready for the April opening. A new roof, the entire outside of the house needed painting, inside rooms needed to be painted and decorated as well, and then there was the landscaping. The list never seemed to end.

Sharon wondered if they would ever be ready to open in time. Yet the new handyman was doing a great job fixing things and painting rooms and all the other projects that needed to be done. They might make it yet.

For a man in his fifties, he sure took care of himself. Those muscles and dark ebony eyes kept getting in the way of her being able to concentrate and direct him. It was a good thing Jason knew what had to be done and just did it with little supervision. Now, if only he could cook.

Janice entered the kitchen, where Sharon was stacking dishes on the shelves.

"We've got to do something about a cook as soon as we can. You know we have enough to do with the administration and hosting. Since day one, that's been a high priority on our list."

Janice sighed. "I talked to Joe at the cafe and asked him if he knew of anyone who may help. He gave me a name, but when I called her, she said it would be too much."

"Well, I'm getting worried. Time is marching on, and we can't open without a cook. Do we put an ad in the paper again?"

"God supplied our needs the last time we placed an ad. He will do it again. He is so faithful," asked Sharon.

"No, I think we need to go farther away. We must have a professional if we are going to please our guests. We're charging a pretty penny for the time they spend here. Everything must be first class! We need someone who will not only make healthy meals, but they need to be delectable and appealing!"

"Well, we need to do something P.D.Q.!" replied Sharon.

Jason overheard the ladies discussing the hiring of a cook and interrupted.

"I don't know whether you would be interested or not, but my younger brother Raymond has been a Chef in the Hotel Industry for years," shared Jason.

"A while back, he told me that he was getting tired of the rat race and was thinking of looking for something a little less stressful. Would you like me to contact him to see if he would be interested?"

Sharon spoke up, "That would be great! Have him come up here so he can meet us so we can check out his credentials. If he's single, he could share the Boathouse with you, if you don't mind. This would be wonderful. We can then move ahead even faster than we anticipated. God is so good."

Jason contacted his brother Raymond, and he agreed to come up the following week to see the layout of the facility and have an interview with Janice and Sharon. Jason was looking forward to seeing Raymond again. It had been a while. Having him here will also help to cover up some of his time away to work undercover on this case. This would work out perfectly. I need a break in this case to find out what the connection is with the farmers who were murdered.

Raymond arrived for his interview, and Janice couldn't get over how the dark-haired, blue-eyed brother looked so much like Jason yet had a difference about him. One had dark eyes, the other light. He seemed shyer than Jason, and she found that to be very charming.

Janice and Sharon showed Raymond around and interviewed him as they toured the new kitchen. It was thoroughly modernized, and he was very excited about all the improvements, especially the new, up-to-date equipment that had been installed in the kitchen. The state-of-the-art stove was something that made him want to create the most delicious and appetizing meals he could ever prepare.

Even the decor, with all the stainless-steel appliances and up-to-date cabinetry, made Raymond feel like he could be the 'King of the Kitchen.' He sure hoped they would hire him!

"Janice, why don't you show Raymond the Boathouse?" suggested Sharon.

"Sure Sharon, I will. Come on, Raymond. I'm sure Jason won't mind."

As they walked to the Boathouse, Raymond thought how attractive Janice was and so petite. There was something about her that made you want to take her in your arms and cuddle and protect her. Where did that come from? Lord, please help me keep my mind on business!

Janice opened the door to the apartment and was surprised at how much Jason had done. It was so clean! What an improvement!

"What do you think? Your brother has done an amazing job. I haven't been up here since the first day we showed it to him. Wow!"

"That's Jason for you. He likes everything clean and in its place! I'm sure we could both live here very comfortably."

"Let's go talk to Sharon. Do you think you would like to come and work for us?"

"I think it would be great for me, and I believe I could satisfy all your needs," replied Raymond.

Janice smiled and thought that was great, but there is only one who can do that, and it's not a man.

Raymond was hired, and it was agreed that he would arrive two weeks before opening to settle in and prepare menus. Janice was looking forward to that time with quite a bit of excitement. He was very nice!

~~~~~~

All of Jason's days off were consumed with the investigation into the strange murders. For the past three years, each July 1st, there was a murder in this small town. The local Sheriff's Department were scratching their heads trying to solve these murders.

They finally called on the CIA to help with their investigation. Each murder had the same MO. A farmer, poisoned, was left in a weird position in a field on his own farm. So far, they haven't been able to identify the poison or the link between the farmers.

It was going to take some breaks and much prayer to solve this case. They needed to find the link between each murder and the murderer. I need to keep undercover so that no one except the sheriff knows who I am. If the murderer should find out, it could mean danger for the ladies. I do not want to have The Sanctuary involved in any way.

If the ladies suspect anything, that could be a problem. They must not know what I'm doing. If anything happened to either of them, I would never forgive myself! Lord, I need your covering and your wisdom!

It was now two weeks before the official opening, and Raymond had arrived.

I'm looking forward to being away from the hotel industry and fitting into this small community. Janice looks even more attractive than the first time I met her. There's something about that lady that I find very enticing. This will be an interesting venture, he thought.

Raymond entered the Boathouse. It now had twin beds and an extra closet for his clothes. The ladies were very thoughtful. I'm sure Jason had a part in this as well. He's done a great job of getting the whole place in order.

This apartment will be a place to relax after a full day's work. This will be so much better than working in the hotel industry. The owners are very pleasing to the eye. They seem to know what they want, and I'm the man that can give it to them.

Raymond was still lost in thought. 'Now, I'll go to the kitchen to start planning my menus and order supplies. I hope I meet Janice along the way.'

Janice just stepped out the front door as Raymond approached. She had a soft green coat on that matched the green in her eyes. She almost took Raymond's breath away.

"Hi Raymond, how are you settled in? It's a beautiful day isn't it." asked Janice.

"Yes, thanks for the extra bed and closet. That works great! I'm going to take a look at the kitchen. Would you like to come and join me?" replied Raymond.

Janice blushed, "I'll come in a little later. I'm just on my way to do an errand. Thanks for asking Raymond. See you later then."

What is it about this man that gives me this strange feeling in the pit of my stomach? It's not bad, it's quite exciting, but I have never felt like this before.

Raymond noticed the blush. She certainly is a real looker, and her charm is shyness, which I like very much. Maybe, just maybe, this would be a place where I might find true romance and relationship. I'm a little tired of playing the field.

Janice drove into town thinking about Raymond. I find him very nice, and those heavenly blues get me every time. This strange feeling in my stomach is increasing. I don't think it's bad, but I need to talk to Sharon to make sure. "Lord, please help me walk close to you, and I sure could use some understanding!"

Everything was beginning to take shape. The charm of The Sanctuary is the setting on the lake and the beautiful building that stands out from the road and the lake. Part of the beauty is its positioning on the property, which gives a fabulous view of the lake from the front and the back of the house. The two-story dwelling has been finally preserved and restored to its original beauty.

The completion of the wraparound veranda looks like an old Victorian mansion. The white wicker furniture, now grouped for couples, groups, or the ones who would like to have some time alone looks truly inviting. The grounds have all been prepared, and the tulips, daffodils, and lilac bushes are all in full bloom.

The welcoming sign at the end of the driveway indicated that The Sanctuary Retreat Center was right ahead and began the journey up the long drive.

Guests would be able to feel the serenity of the property as soon as they drive in and feel the beautiful peace as they walk or drive throughout the whole of the property. The perfect elements that would ensure our guests would want to come back time and time again.

~~~~

Sharon was working in the office and decided to call her son, Daniel. It's time we have him bring Casey up so he can become familiar with the place before the guests arrive. Casey is Sharon's beautiful Collie. He has a mix of black, soft brown, and white in his coat, with a black mask from the top of his head to the tip of his nose. He is eight years old and loves people.

Janice came from the kitchen. "How are things going, Sharon?"

"I just called Daniel. He's bringing Casey on Friday. I can't wait to see him. I've missed him so much."

"Great, Jason and Raymond have fixed a lovely, warm spot for him in the Boathouse. Do you think he will be all right up there?" asked Janice.

"Yes, he's never been a dog that lived in the house; he's only visited! He had a spot in the garage with a dog hole to come in and out as he pleased. He'll be fine and happy to see me, I'm sure!"

Friday arrived, and so did Casey. He ran to Sharon as Daniel opened the car door and just about knocked her over. They both were so glad to see each other.

"Casey, you look beautiful. Thanks so much, Daniel, my wonderful son, for bringing him. I've missed him so much!"

"Wow, Mom, the place is looking really great. You have all done fantastic work!" replied Daniel with excitement.

"It is looking good, isn't it? Come on, and I'll show you around! You can meet Jason and Raymond. They have been such a great help! God has been so good in providing our every need!"

After they toured the house and grounds, Raymond threw together a great meal for all of them to enjoy before Daniel had to go back to work.

"I'm so sorry I can't stay. I must get back to my office. It's getting so busy as people are starting to book their summer holidays already. You can be assured I will make some time to come back and enjoy all that you have here. By the way, Raymond, a fantastic meal. You are going to be a hit with the guests!" commented Daniel.

Casey warmed up to Jason quickly, like a long-lost friend. So, Jason took him to the boathouse to get Casey settled into his new home. "Well, boy, I hope you like it here. We're going to have a great time!"

Casey just about turned himself inside out as he wagged his tail and licked Jason's hands. We're going to make a great team together!

It was only a few days before the official opening, and all the rooms were booked. Not one of the six rooms that were ready for guests would be vacant. What a wonderful beginning.

Just a few finishing touches here and there were needed. Fresh flowers for the reception area and Dining Room. Guest rooms are to be checked for any last-minute additions. Every detail throughout is perfect and in order. It was looking good, and Janice and Sharon were excited and couldn't wait for their guests to arrive. We were also getting to know and enjoy the sense of humor and work ethic of both brothers.

Janice decided to take the hedge clippers and do a little cleaning of some of the hedges at the back of the house.

It wouldn't take long, and she'd have it done before Sharon noticed she was doing it. She was thinking of how Sharon hated her handling the power tools when it suddenly slipped and caught Janice's finger. The cut was deep.

She turned off the clippers and held her finger; there was blood everywhere. Quickly, she ran in through the back door and just happened to ran face-to-face into Sharon. Oh no!

"Janice, what have you done now? It looks like you are going to need stitches. Come on, I'll take you to Dr. Philips. You make me so mad. How many times have I told you not to use the power tools? You make me nervous, and now you can see why!" scolded Sharon. She grabbed a towel and yelled at Jason that she was off to take Janice to the doctor in town. They arrived at the Doctor's office, and the nurse took them right in.

"Well, Janice, let's see what you have done. This takes me back to when you were younger. I remember your visits with your mother throughout the summer months! Do you remember when you were swinging on the rope from one tree to another and fell and broke your arm?" asked the doctor.

"Oh yes, I remember it well. It was the last of my swinging days! One of these days, I'll learn, I'm sure!"

"You only need a few stitches, and it will be fine! We had better give you a Tetanus shot, though, ok!" suggested the doctor.

Janice sighed and braced herself as she said, "I hate needles!"

~~~

Janice and Sharon arrived back at The Sanctuary to find Raymond trying out a new dish. He asked them and Jason if they would like to try it for dinner. He looked at Janice's finger, all bandaged up, and said, "I'll cut your food up for you if you need help!"

Janice gave him a look, "I can cut up my own food thank you!"

They all arrived in the kitchen at six o'clock. To their surprise, Raymond had placed a tablecloth on the counter and set the table as if it were an elegant dinner.

Jason laughed, "Who're you trying to impress, buddy? I'm sure it isn't me!"

Raymond blushed. "I just wanted to show you I can set a mean table as well as be a great cook!"

They all laughed, and the atmosphere was friendly and comfortable. They were getting to know each other, and there was the real feeling of a family working together and having a good time.

Sharon was the first to compliment him on the dinner. "You have outdone yourself, Raymond! You're going to have the guests eating out of your hands."

"I would rather have them eating off the plates, but thanks. I must admit it's a good recipe, and I'll definitely use it for the guests. Now I have a special dessert as well. You must close your eyes as I bring it to the table."

Raymond took a minute and then came back to the table.

"Okay, open your eyes!"

To their surprise, he had prepared a Baked Alaska, and it was burning bright as they opened their eyes.

"Okay, enough showing off! You're trying to be teacher's pet and I'll have to do one up on you now!" exclaimed Jason in jest.

Janice was rubbing her stomach. "I'm so full, but you can cook for me anytime. If you want to remain a friend, though, you'll have to cut down on the calories."

"This was a special dinner because we've all been working so hard. I felt everyone needed a break. I'll be much more calorie-conscious with the guests."

Everyone pitched in to clean up. The camaraderie and joking ended the evening, with each one going off to bed full and content. Janice hadn't had time to mention to Sharon how she was reacting to Raymond, so she decided this would be a good time.

"Sharon, I'm not sure what is happening with me, but every time I'm near Raymond, I get a strange feeling in my stomach, almost like butterflies! It's so strange, and I blush as well!"

"Oh Janice, you silly goose, you're attracted to him and you're feeling it deep inside. I'm sorry; I didn't mean to call you a silly goose, but you are so cute and naive. It's okay! Just enjoy it and let the relationship take its natural course."

"Well, I'm so new at this! When I was in Africa, I was busy doing God's work, and I didn't have any time for romance. I haven't a clue what to do or how to handle it!"

"You'll be fine! If you have any questions, you know I'm here for you. Now, let's get some sleep! We only have two more full days to get everything done!"

~~~

The following day, Jason made up an excuse to go into town for fertilizer for the lawns so he could meet with Sheriff Fisher. It had been a few days since they had any conversation. *I need to get moving and look for some answers.* He met the Sheriff at Joe's Cafe.

"Hi Joe, I'll have a coffee and a piece of Tori's delicious apple pie with some of that cheddar cheese. You're certainly blessed to have a woman who is such a good cook. She's great with your customers too! You are doubly blessed, man!"

Sheriff Fisher came in and sat with Jason. It appeared that these two men were becoming friends. There could be no link to the murders between the two of them. Meeting at the cafe as friends was a good cover.

"Is there any news coming forth?" asked the Sheriff.

"We have found that all these farmers had been friends for years. They played poker every other week at Walter Thompson's place. There is definitely some connection. We now must find out what it was."

Jason arrived back at the Sanctuary, thankful that they at least had something to go on at last. I don't want Janice and Sharon to get suspicious of my time away. It could be very dangerous if my cover is blown. Help me, Lord, to be wise!

There was a lot of commotion when he got back. Casey had run off and chased a skunk and, of course, got sprayed. No one wanted to touch him or let him inside. Jason called him and asked Raymond to get lots of tomato juice and a couple of pairs of rubber gloves to bathe him. He took him to the bathroom in the Boathouse. Raymond came running with the tomato juice. Casey looked so sad, and it was hard for the two men to keep him in the tub. They finally got him covered in the tomato juice, rinsed him off, and then dried him.

Then soaked him in more tomato juice and rinsed him off again as the aroma of Casey was still quite strong. He still had the small odor of skunk that would leave him in time, but after this ordeal, he was tired but much happier.

As Jason finished the task, he gave Casey a hug. "You won't want to be chasing any more of those little critters, now will you boy!" Casey while wagging his tail sat as Jason's feet, as he wagged his tail finally content.

"I'll go back to the kitchen and get some cleaner and freshener to clean up the bathroom. Open the window to get that smell out of here or we won't be able to sleep here tonight. We really needed this so close to opening!" commented Raymond.

Jason laughed. "You're not kidding. We may have to use clothes pegs to sleep tonight, but at least he's clean. I know of a mixture to clean him up if we didn't get it all."

~~~

April Fifteenth blossomed forth with the fragrance of the lilacs in full force. It was a beautiful sunny and warm day for so early in the season! The Sanctuary and staff were completely ready for their guests.

Mr. and Mrs. Chambers from Toronto were the first to arrive. "What a beautiful place you have here! We felt the peace as we drove up your beautiful driveway," they commented.

"You are the first to arrive and have the honor of being our very first guests. Come and let me show you to your room! Jason will bring up your bags shortly," replied Sharon.

Sharon escorted them into The Peace Room; Mrs. Chambers stopped and exclaimed! "This room has been well named. I can feel the peace of the Lord here."

"The lavender scent you chose is quite calming, and I love the pine furniture. It's beautiful, and the view of the lake is breathtaking. Oh, George, let's go for a walk. We can unpack later."

Sharon was so pleased. I hope that all the guests will be this enthusiastic. She thought.

Another car drove up, and a very pretty young woman stepped out of her car. Janice was out the door to greet her.

"Welcome, you must be Miss Chesterfield. Please follow me, and we will bring your bags up for you soon."

"It's lovely here. I have been looking forward to my stay. This is going to be a beautiful resting place."

When she saw the Princess Room all in white with lace, embroidered linens, and a four-poster bed draped with crisp white netting and lots of fresh green plants, she oohed and awed.

"This is beautiful. I feel like a princess! You have done a beautiful job in decorating."

"I can't take credit for the decorating. My partner Sharon is the decorator. She'll be so pleased to hear you like it. We'll have your luggage up in no time. There are hot and cold drinks in the Lounge. You are welcome to go there any time during your stay with us. Please make yourself at home."

Janice met Sharon, who had just shown the Petersons to their room. The Petersons were so happy with the Sunset Room. She raved about the pink, blue, and orange theme. She said it reminded her of a beautiful sunset. Her husband liked the oak furniture. Apparently, he is a lover of wood and hates to see it painted.

"You must be thrilled at the reaction of the guests. They can't say enough about the decor!" asked Janice.

"I'm so excited! This is such a great beginning!" replied Sharon.

They heard the sound of two cars pulling in and went out to meet them. A huge black limo was depositing a couple at the door.

Sharon moved forward to greet them.

"Welcome to The Sanctuary. You must be the Pendleton's from England! Your chauffeur can leave your bags on the veranda. Our man will bring them up for you."

"No, thank you. He can bring them up before he leaves."

"All right, then, would you follow me?"

Sharon hoped they were going to be happy in The Abby Room. I sure hope I picked this right, but when they entered the room, Mrs. Pendleton exclaimed, "This is so much like our bedroom at home. You even have the beige and browns that Peter loves. We love the mahogany bed and dressers. You couldn't have picked a better room for us. Could she, Peter?"

Peter cleared his throat, "It will be just fine, Matilda, just fine!"

Janice had shown the young newlyweds from Nebraska to the Sun Rise room. She met Sharon at the Reception area.

"Well, the Frasers are settling in their room. They love the colors. She said they would wake up every morning with an expectancy of good things to come. She was particularly thrilled with the splashes of white daisies on the spreads and curtains.

"Mr. Fraser wasn't sure about the wicker furniture, but she was so delighted he had to give in. When we decorate the additional rooms, we better make them a little more masculine." Suggested Janice.

"I've done them half and half, but I see what you're saying. We can't put a six-foot-something guy into a frilly room with white wicker," replied Sharon laughing.

They had one more guest to arrive, Tom Jackson from Vancouver. He would be in the Georgian Room. The soft blues on the walls and linens complimented the cherry wood furniture. It should be masculine enough for him unless he is a lumberjack.

It was mid-afternoon before he arrived. He was a good-looking outdoorsman type. He was quite happy with the room and was looking forward to getting out on the lake.

Some of the guests had walked down to the dock and sat on the Adirondack chairs by the water. Others had gathered in the Lounge. They were enjoying the relaxed atmosphere of the huge room. It was filled with black leather couches and chairs. There was a beautiful stone fireplace that was lit to bring that cozy atmosphere to the Lounge.

The walls were painted in a dove grey, and matching curtains completed the pleasing decor. The fresh yellow daisies brought a breath of spring to the room. It was a delightful and cozy place to relax, play board games or read.

The delicious aromas coming from the kitchen were making all the guests eager for their first dinner at The Sanctuary. Many were very hungry as they had traveled from a great distance. It was finally time to sit down for dinner.

The Dining Room, facing the Lake, was painted in soft blue to reflect the beauty of the lake and sky. The tables were covered in white linen cloths, and the white wicker chairs were upholstered in blue linen that complimented the shade on the walls. A vase of white daisies centered on each table brought a touch of Summer that was delightful.

The dishes were white with delphinium blue edging, and the silverware was an old Rogers Brothers pattern called Daffodil. Blue linen serviettes picked up the edging from the dishes and were tucked in the sparkling Kosta crystal glasses like fans, completing the elegant setting. It was breathtaking as the guests came in to sit at the tables.

Raymond had prepared a scrumptious meal, beginning with a choice of shrimp cocktail or mixed fruit compote. He followed this with a cold cucumber soup that was quite tangy but delicious.

The main course was roast beef cooked to perfection, guaranteed to melt in the mouth, with roast potatoes, creamed turnip, green beans almandine, Yorkshire pudding, and, of course, horseradish for those who like that tangy lift with their roast beef. Dessert was delicious Dutch apple pie a la mode. Delectable coffees and assorted teas finished the feast.

All the guests were thrilled with the decor, ambiance, and food. As each one left the Dining Room, the comment was, "Delicious, can't wait until tomorrow to taste the next meals prepared by the Chef."

Janice and Sharon quickly looked after cleaning up the Dining Room so that they could get on with their evening.

"Well, Sharon, if this is a sample of what we have to look forward to, I am overjoyed and very pleased!" said Janice.

"Yes, let's get these dishes in the Dishwasher and enjoy the rest of our evening."

"What do you think about taking a walk down to the Dock?" suggested Sharon.

"Sounds good to me, let's hurry," replied Janice excitedly.

As they walked to the dock, they noticed Jason's car was gone again. "He seems to be gone from here whenever he's not on duty. Do you think he has a girlfriend in town or something?" asked Sharon.

"Who knows? It really isn't any of our business unless you are interested in him or his whereabouts when he's off duty!" replied Janice.

Sharon's face reddened at Janice's remark, and she became very quiet. Janice was so thankful to the Lord for all He had done for them.

"The Lord has been so good in giving us Jason and Raymond to help get this place in order. They are not only capable but kind of nice to have around, if you know what I mean!"

"Know what you mean?" asked Sharon.

"You know that I know what I mean! If Raymond gets very close to me, I'm like a bowl of jelly. He must think I'm mental. My words get all jumbled up, and sometimes I even stutter." exclaimed Janice.

Sharon laughed. "Well, bowl of jelly, here he is now!"

As they approached the lake and looked at the beautiful sunset, Raymond came up to them.

"Well, ladies", asked Raymond, "What do you feel about your first day with guests? Are you pleased with everything and everyone?"

Janice spoke up first. "We are so pleased with everything. You and Jason have done so much to make The Sanctuary a home away from home. His handy work around the place and your cooking skills have added so much. You certainly earn your wages beyond the call of duty. Thank you so much from the bottom of our hearts!"

"It's our pleasure to help you ladies out on this venture. It's going to take a lot of your time. Jason and I both hope that you'll have some leisure time so we can get to know you better. The last two weeks have been great, but we've all been so busy that there hasn't been time to get to know each other at all."

Both Janice and Sharon looked surprised and pleased with Raymond's remark. "We would certainly like to take time to get to know both you and Jason, and we assure you we will make the time. All work and no play will make us all very dull," quipped Sharon.

Raymond smirked, "We certainly couldn't have dull hostesses and employees guiding our guests now, could we?"

As they were finishing their conversation, Jason drove in and jumped out of his car. He looked so handsome that Sharon's heart did a little flutter, and she thought she had better try to tuck any feelings of attraction away so they wouldn't interfere with their working relationship here at The Sanctuary.

They all talked together for a while, enjoying the sunset and the beauty of the lake. The sunset shining down on the crystal-clear water was breathtaking. Soon, they decided that it was time to go in to see if the guests needed anything. As the ladies walked away, they heard Jason say, "You know, those are two of the prettiest gals I have seen in a long time!"

They smiled at each other, and there was a little more lift to their steps as they hurried to make certain everyone was content before going to bed.

Jason had to go into town to purchase wood to do some work on the dock, so he took time to meet with the Sheriff. They chose to meet at Joe's Cafe again so that it looked like it was a chance meeting. It was risky to spend too much time at the Sheriff's office. He was so concerned that his cover would be blown.

I figure it would be all right if I'm seen with the Sheriff. After all, as an employee of The Sanctuary, it's important that I build relationships with all the locals in the town.

As they sat and talked, Jason realized the Sheriff was weighed down with the murders of the local farmers.

"I just don't know what's going to happen if we don't get this solved quickly. Everyone here is on tenterhooks, wondering what's going to happen this year. I sure hope that you can help us catch the murderer or murderers!"

Jason shook his head. "It certainly is bewildering in a quiet place like this. Someone must have a vendetta of some sort. This needs to be solved! We must catch whoever is responsible."

Janice picked up the car keys, "We need some groceries, so I am going to go into town." She drove by Joe's Cafe and noticed Jason sitting in the window with the sheriff. She wondered what he was doing with the sheriff.

She hurried along, bought the groceries, and then headed back home. On the way back, she offered up a quick prayer.

'Lord, please don't let anything interfere with his working at The Sanctuary.'

Janice began to be very suspicious of Jason's absence from The Sanctuary. He is away quite often. When she arrived, she sought Sharon out, "Sharon, I saw Jason sitting with the Sheriff in Joe's Cafe. Why would he be spending time with the Sheriff? It just doesn't feel right to me. Do you think we should question him about it?"

"No, I think we have to have a little more faith in him. Let's see if he mentions the Sheriff in his conversations. Besides, he said he wants to make friends with the locals. It makes better business when he needs a favour."

Janice took the groceries into the kitchen where Raymond was preparing the evening meal. He smiled, "Well Janice, I see you did lots of shopping. It looks like you have everything on my list. You are wonderful!"

Janice blushed, "It's all part of my job!" She quickly turned and walked away with thoughts that she shouldn't have sounded so harsh. She needed to lighten up a little.

Raymond thought, 'Oh, I think I had better tread lightly here. I certainly don't want to blow it. She is one lady I would like to get to know and be able to break through that shyness! Lord, help me to work through this and to have patience, especially with Janice.'

So far, the guests were all loving their stay and sharing their comments with Sharon and Janice.

"Well, you can be assured we'll be telling all our friends and relatives about this place. You have truly made it a Sanctuary and the food has been more delicious than we could ever imagine."

Sharon and Janice were so pleased with the response of the guests. They were standing together in the Reception Area. Sharon was shuffling some papers and looked up to see Miss Chesterfield and Mr. Jackson walking by.

"Is something happening between those two? They have been doing a lot together ever since the first evening," commented Sharon.

Janice smiled, "Romance seems to be in the air. Let's hope it isn't a summer fling. Even though he's an American and she's Canadian, Seattle and Vancouver aren't so far apart."

"Hey Janice, I believe you're becoming a romantic!"

Blushing she replied "Maybe I am. There may be hope for me yet!"

~~~~~

Jason was so thankful to have Raymond on site.

He could help with excuses if there were questions about where Jason was or where he was going. He felt the ladies were pretty acute and may begin to wonder about his absence from the property. It was a little more difficult to get away as most of the errands into town were becoming less and less frequent. The Lord would really have to give him the wisdom so that there was no possible link to the murderer and The Sanctuary.

The week was just about finished, and all the guests would be leaving on Saturday with new guests arriving on Sunday. There was so much to do in such a short time. The beds all have to be changed, rooms and bathrooms cleaned and the laundry to be done.

Sharon and Janice were discussing the work ahead "Well Janice, we are going to have a lot to do in one day. I sure hope and pray that we can get it all done in time for the new guests!"

"It does sound like a lot of work, but what if we buy a second set of sheets for each bed so we don't have to wait for the washing and drying of the sheets before we can do the changing of the beds. That way we can put a new set of sheets on each bed as soon as we strip them which will save us time and stress on departure day. We can order them online and also save time rather than drive into town. What do you think?" replied Janice.

"That sounds like a great idea Janice. Why don't we do that now then we may have them by Friday if they are in stock. That will save time. We can do all the laundry on Monday leaving our weekend not as stressful as it needs to be. Let's do that now."

"I'm also going to ask Raymond to do the grocery shopping for the week on Fridays, so we can get all the inside work done by the weekend. Then on Saturday we can concentrate on room clean up and beds." suggested Janice.

"That way there will be less inside work for Jason to do. He can then concentrate on all of his outside duties like checking the boats, outside cleanup, and getting the outside lawns done in time for our new guests." replied Janice. "We can try it out and see how it goes."

Jason arrived back at the Sanctuary after his meeting with the Sheriff. He had a little more to go on now. At least there seemed to be a dim light being shed on the murders. All the farmers had been friends for years so there had to be a connection. What was it?

There was only one more in the group of farmer friends still living. A visit to him was next on Jason's list. As soon as he had time, he would be having a little visit and talk with him. His name was Paul Ashton and he had been part of the group that had played poker together for at least 25 years.

Janice was sitting on the front veranda enjoying a nice hot cup of tea. She had asked Sharon to join her and was waiting to have some time for the two of them to share some of their thoughts about the week. Sharon came out on the porch with a hot cup of Green Tea laced with lemon, and of course a Butter Tart, her favourite.

"Well, my friend, this has certainly been a busy week, but a very rewarding one. The guests have enjoyed their stay and are booking for next year already. The Chambers from Toronto have booked for the last weekend in August. They said, they have not had a holiday like this in years!"

Janice spoke softly, "On rethinking the workload, I feel maybe, we are going to have to hire more help. We need a girl to help with housekeeping and someone else to help in the kitchen. Let's see if we can get some local help through the church this Sunday."

~~~

Jason and Raymond came up from the Boat House looking like two of the handsomest and most desirable men you could ever dream of meeting. To think they could look this good in their fifties. What did they look like when they were in their twenties?

Sharon's heart began to flutter as Jason stepped on to the veranda. "Will you two have a drink of something with us?"

Both men jumped at the offer, "If there's any coffee left in the Reception Room, we would love a pick-me-up and a little time to take it easy." Janice got up to get the drinks, with Raymond following right along behind her.

Jason came and sat by Sharon looking deep into her baby blues. "The week has gone well, don't you think?" asked Jason.

Sharon tried to get her heart to stop fluttering, but her face became a bright pink and the palm of her hands became sweaty.

~~~

"It has been a wonderful week and you two have added so much to our efforts here. We are so thankful that God sent you, our way. You have truly been just what we needed in every way!"

Raymond and Janice came back, carrying a plate of goodies from the pantry. They all sat and enjoyed each other's company, with the added bonus of the baked goods. Hmm Hmm Good!

They sat for quite a while as the sun set once again on the Lake bringing about a stillness that was only broken with the familiar sound of the Loons coming from across the water. It was so peaceful, no one really wanted to move, but Raymond was the first to get up.

"I need to get to bed early as I want to prepare a very special breakfast for the guests last day tomorrow!"

Janice also turned in, leaving Sharon and Jason alone on the veranda. Sharon started to pick up the dishes and Jason jumped up, "Let me help with those."

As their hands slightly touched, little sparks were not only visible in their eyes, but they both felt them right through to the core of their being. They both realized that there was a definite attraction to each other and knew they had better play it cool. Working together was hard enough without these kinds of emotions getting in the way.

Jason knew he needed all his wits and time to spend on the murder case. After all that was why he was in this area. He needed to get the job done before another farmer ended up as a scarecrow in his own field. That had been the final humiliation the murderer had concocted. He dressed the victims up like scarecrows and hung them up in their own fields on poles to look like a human scarecrow. You had to be strong to be able to lift 150-200 pounds of dead weight.

~~~

The next day the guests had all checked out and left for home and Sharon and Janice were busy with the housekeeping, while Raymond finished up in the kitchen. Later, the four of them would share a dinner that Raymond had prepared. It would be a nice time for them to get together and learn more about each other.

The meal was delicious as usual. Raymond had prepared a pasta dish with shrimp and a yummy cream sauce. An interesting romaine lettuce salad with oranges, and toasted slivered almonds. A garnish of green onion and tangy dressing to give it a lift that satisfied the palette of the most critical diner. For dessert he had made a rhubarb custard pie with a high meringue topping baked to a golden brown.

The relationship between the four was becoming chatty and comfortable "Janice, why don't you tell us about your time in Africa?" asked Jason.

~~~

"Oh, I don't know! I wouldn't know where to start or what to share with you."

"Tell us what you did there, come on! It's interesting," suggested Sharon.

"Ok, well I worked with children mostly. Teaching them English and stories from the Bible. I was able to lead many of them to the Lord. I loved each of them as if they were my own. It was a hard time but rewarding. Having to live on very little food and trusting God for everything was a major part of everyday life! To have what we have now makes me very humble and thankful!"

"Janice had to leave Africa because her parents were killed in an accident here in Ontario. Can I tell them about it, or will it upset you too much?" asked Sharon.

Janice said, "No, go ahead. It's easier if you tell it!"

"Some boys started an old car and placed a board under the gas pedal so that the car would drive along the road at 70 miles an hour. Then they watched where the car would go. They thought they were ingenious. They never expected that someone would be driving along the road at that time of night. Normally, there wouldn't have been, but the Rogers had decided to take a different way home that night and ran into the man less car. Janice had to come home to bury her parents, and then be involved in the investigations of their deaths. I was so glad to be able to be with her during the trial and the aftermath of it all."

The men were very taken back; Raymond took Janice's hand "I'm so sorry. I had no idea what you've been through. How are you now?"

"It's been three years, so I am pretty good now, but when I think back on it, I think of the waste."

~~~

"Both of their lives and those young boys. I was so glad that I had Sharon to be such a support during that difficult time. She was a real pillar of strength for me as I have no other family. Her family has been like my own!" She has been like a sister to me.

Raymond said, "God is good! Isn't it amazing how He brings people into situations to help us when we are alone. He knows our needs and meets them."

The group was very quiet as they cleaned up the kitchen. Each lost in their own thoughts and memories of their own past. Sharon was feeling the sadness among them "Can we pray together so that we might go off to bed in a peaceful manner?"

After the prayer, they all felt better, and Sharon headed for the office to check some last-minute details for the incoming guest's tomorrow. Jason was close behind her and touched her shoulder.

~~~

Once again, the sparks ignited. As she turned and investigated those deep pools, she became lost. "I know there's a very strong attraction between us and I don't know what you think about it. I am trying to keep it cool but whenever you're near I became like a weak puppy. I believe you are feeling this attraction as much as I am."

She drew her breath in, "I have been a widow for five years and felt that I would never feel anything for a man again. I loved Bill very much. When Bill died, I felt I was dead inside, but I admit there is a very strong attraction to you, but I have so many questions about you. You don't share much about yourself or past relationships. It makes me very nervous."

He looked at her and knew he would have to share some things with her. "Can we find some time to talk together privately?"

As she stepped away, she replied, "As soon as I can juggle it, we'll meet, I will let you know..Until then, we need to play this cool, don't you agree?"

"By all means, that's what I have been trying to do." Jason then left to check the grounds and dock before retiring to the Boat House.

The following morning, they all drove to the local church. Sharon and Janice loved the pastor. He was round and jolly, and his sermons were like an arrow that went directly to the heart. As Sharon thought about him and laughed. "You are going to love Pastor David. He has such a wonderful sense of humor, and his messages are deep!"

Jason spoke up, "I've heard him a couple of times before I moved to The Sanctuary. He seems like a great guy!"

When they drove up to the church, Janice spotted Martha Alexander and her daughter Toni. "Let's go and speak to them about working with us."

"Martha, can we speak to you?" asked Janice.

Martha stopped. "Sharon and I were wondering whether you and Toni might be interested in coming to work with us at The Sanctuary?"

"Your timing couldn't be better, replied Martha. We were just talking to Pastor David about needing work as my husband Steve was laid off awhile back, and hasn't been able to find work here!"

They went over all the details between them, and Martha and Toni were able to start the following day. Janice looked at Sharon, "I can't believe how everything for us has worked out ahead of time! Now we have our added help!"

"God is good!"

～～～

It was Tuesday before Jason was able to visit Paul Ashton's farm. Driving along the road to the farm he was praying, 'Lord, I need your help and your wisdom to solve these murders, let there be something here that I can grab hold of, to move along in this case. What connection, if any, does he have with the murder victims?'

Upon arriving he found Mr. Ashton in the barn. He approached him and put out his hand to shake his, "I'm Jason Morris and I'm helping Sheriff Fisher with the murder of your friends. Do you know of anyone who would have not only poisoned your friends but had the wicked sense of humor to hang them up like scarecrows?"

~~~~~

Ashton shook his head, "I have tried and tried to think of anyone we have cheated or done something to that would cause them to take out such vengeance like this. I cannot think of anyone. It must be a man, or two people, to have put each of them on stakes like scarecrows."

Jason scratched his head, "We are baffled unless you can come up with someone. There must be someone in your past that hates you this much. You do realize that you are the last of your poker group?"

"Of course I do. Why do you think I 've been trying to remember something that would come to the light? I know that July 1st is coming too quickly. I'll try and think back some more and if I think of anyone, I'll call you immediately."

Driving away Jason looked back at Paul Ashton's face. He could see the fear deep within his eyes. A break is needed soon, or we'll have another murder on our hands. We'll have to post someone around the clock for his protection as the time draws near.

~~~~~

Martha and Toni fit in at The Sanctuary as if they had been there since the beginning. Sharon and Janice were finding that they helped take a lot of the load off them. Sharon was particularly pleased as they were able to fill in wherever they were needed. It felt so good to be able to hire mother and daughter from their local church. It was great having people of like minds working together. They all shared the same faith and enjoyed working together.

Janice was doing some small repairs to some shelving in the Kitchen and stepped off the ladder. She was about to fall when Raymond's two strong arms caught her. She found herself looking right into his beautiful blue eyes.

"You really need to be more careful little lady. You could have been hurt quite badly and then what would we do if you were hobbling around on crutches?" commented Raymond.

~~~~~

Janice was embarrassed, "Well, isn't it good that there was a great big strong man to catch me so that I wouldn't be hobbling around on crutches or whatever." Raymond continued to hold her.

"Well, Prince Charming, are you going to put me down so that we can both get on with our chores or are you just going to stand there with your arms full?" as Raymond slowly put Janice down, he actually gave her a quick hug.

"Sorry, I couldn't help myself; you look really cute when you're mad."

Janice was flustered but felt that strange feeling in the pit of her stomach again. "Thank you, Raymond, I realize I could have been hurt and then I'd be of no use to anyone. I will try not to extend myself when I am doing those little jobs that Jason could do. I just want to alleviate some of his work. He has a lot to do here."

"Well, I know he loves it all. So don't try and help him too much or he might think you are trying to take his job away from him!" replied Raymond.

As Janice took the ladder away, she was frowning but inside there was a smile on her heart. That man sure knows how to get under my skin but I must admit he is attractive and nice and a very good cook and everything a gal would want in a guy. Janice sighed.

Paul Ashton had been trying to figure out who was killing all his friends. Ever since Walter Thompson had died, his friends had been knocked off one by one, each July 1st for the past three years.

Suddenly it hit him, Lorna Thompson. Could this have any connection? How could he even bring this to the police? Could he be convicted of something that happened twenty-five years ago when they were just young guys, and a little wild? It seemed like this was a possibility but how could she ever hang them up to be scarecrows in their own fields. She couldn't possibly be that strong, or was she? He hadn't thought of her or seen her for years. Maybe she had an accomplice. He will definitely have to talk to Jason Morris before it was his turn to be strung up.

Jason could not get out to Paul Ashton's farm fast enough after the call from Paul Ashton sharing that he might have some information pertinent to the murders. I need a valid excuse to go out Jason thought. I hate this deception but what else can I do. He would ask Raymond.

"I have to go out on this case, and I need a reason, like a distraction to not bring suspicion for the girls. Any idea bro?"

"It isn't my time off and I know the ladies are going to be suspicious. Do you need anything urgent in town?" asked Jason.

"This is getting tricky brother! I do need extra eggs for the dessert I'm making for dinner, but you'll need to be back by two! Ok."

"I'll be back just cover me!"

When Jason arrived at the Ashton farm, Paul came out of the barn and hurried toward him. "First off, I want to know if something I did twenty-five years ago could put me in jail now?"

"That all depends on what it was. There are statues of limitations on some crimes but if it was murder, you will still have to be charged. You better own up Paul, if you think this has anything to do with the murder of your friends, and your possible death."

"Well Walter Thompson had an adopted daughter named Lorna that he abused all the time. One night when we all had been drinking and playing poker Lorna came into the room. She was only fourteen at the time but had the figure of an eighteen-year-old. We were kidding and joking around with her, and Walter offered her up to us.

We took four pieces of straw and made them different sizes. The longest straw went first and the rest of us followed, mine being the shortest straw, I was last. We all raped her." Paul said.

Jason looked at the man in unbelief and disgust but realized this could be the revenge of the girl, but how? "Ashton, I don't know how she could pull it off. The fact that each farmer has been set up as a scarecrow could relate back to the order of each straw each of you drew!" "Paul, what order were the straws drawn?" asked Jason.

~~~~~

Paul Ashton's face went white at Jason's remarks. "This could be the link we need to solve these murders."

Paul hesitated with emotion but spoke, "The men were murdered in the order of the straws drawn. My straw was the shortest and I was the last one to rape Lorna, so I am the last one to die."

"Don't worry Paul, we are on top of this. I can do some investigating and see where Lorna was last seen and where she is now. Don't be afraid, you will be protected and out of danger. This is a great clue. Let's hope that this is the right one to solve these murders." Replied Jason. "We will get Headquarters to check her out."

Sharon felt everything was running smoothly at The Sanctuary, but she was becoming very suspicious of Jason's time away.

~~~~~

'As soon as he finishes his work, he is off in his car again,' thought Sharon. 'He is even missing meals here. We really need to have that talk that we were supposed to have with him. I'm going to try and make time this evening to get him alone and talk this out.'

Janice was helping out in the kitchen and Raymond was trying to concentrate on developing a new recipe. It's so hard when Janice is within ten feet of me, he thought. Am I ever going to make any headway with her?

"Janice, would you like to go into town after dinner tonight and take in a movie?"

She was taken back and there was that 'what did Sharon call it, butterflies again'.

~~~~~

"I think that could be arranged after the kitchen is cleaned and ready for breakfast."

"The movie starts at 7:30 so we can just make it if we clean up the kitchen. I can set up for breakfast when we get back if that's ok. What do you say Janice?" asked Raymond.

"All right, sounds good to me!" replied Janice.

The guests that were coming and going at The Sanctuary were all so impressed with the atmosphere, the food and the hospitality, that they were booking for their next visits. Just like their very first guests, they were promising that they would tell their friends and families about this haven.

Sharon was beside herself, "We must get those other three rooms ready so we can take in more guests. We certainly can handle them with our present staff. It'll slow down in the Fall, and we can do some of the renovations then."

Knowing Sharon and how she couldn't wait to put plans into action, Janice said, "We could start slowly now, as long as we don't make any noise or smells to disturb the guests!"

"I don't think we ever thought it would be so successful. We must thank the Lord for bringing Jason and Raymond to us. Then he gave us Martha and Toni. They have all made such a positive addition here!"

"Speaking of Raymond, he has asked me to go into town this evening to a movie. I was surprised when he asked me, but I must admit that I'm a little excited and also apprehensive. This is all new to me. I certainly like what I'm feeling inside!"

~

"Well, it's about time you started thinking a little more about yourself. You have a great time and don't worry about anything here."

Raymond and Janice took off for town and the evening was beautiful. The ease of the conversation was quite surprising to Janice.

"Raymond, thank you for asking me to the movie, I don't take much time for myself, and Sharon is always getting after me to enjoy life more. The years in Africa were great and I enjoyed them but there was never much time for my own pleasures. This is wonderful and I know I am going to enjoy the movie."

"I'm glad that you were open to coming out with me. I can see the shyness in you, and I hope that we can be good friends as well as you being my Boss!"

"Let's not think of my being your Boss, let's work on the friendship part of our relationship first ok," suggested Janice.

They arrived in town and once again Janice noticed Jason's car at the Sheriff's office. She didn't say anything as she did not want to push Raymond to share Jason's secrets.

Jason and Peter Fisher, the Sheriff, had been doing some investigation into the whereabouts of Lorna Thompson. She had left the farm as soon as she turned sixteen. After having several jobs as a waitress, and a grocery salesclerk, she then had some time working in a tree farm and nursery, but then it appeared as if Lorna disappeared and vanished from the planet.

So far, they had not been able to find any evidence of her still being alive. Jason threw up his arms "We really need a break. We only have a short time left before July 1st comes around. If she is the murderer, she has to show up here sometime."

Peter Fisher shook his head "This has to be one of the worst situations we have had here. It isn't making my job easy, and the people are beginning to think I can't do my job. There are rumors that they think it's time for a new Sheriff. We had better get a break in this case soon or I'll be out of a job."

"There must be some trace of her. How could she possibly vanish without a trace? Where did her adoptive mother go? Does she still live in the area? Something must break!"

Sheriff Fisher scratched his head "Yeah, I think the mother moved in with her sister in town."

"All right then, let's get in touch with her and see if she has anything of Lorna's in her possession."

Jason left for The Sanctuary and wondered if he would have a chance to have that talk with Sharon when he got back.

Sharon was sitting on the veranda as he drove up. He parked his car and walked up to her, "Well, I'm glad you are taking a little time for yourself. How're you doing?" he asked.

"I am so pleased with everything here but am wondering when we can have that talk, we were supposed to have," asked Sharon.

"That's great, I was thinking the same thing as I was driving back home. Would you like to take a little stroll down to the dock area where we can have some privacy?"

"That sounds good, it's such a lovely night and I love to hear the loons."

As they walked down the path, Jason put his hand on the small of Sharon's back. She was startled but did not pull away.

It felt nice to have that protection from a man once again.

"Let's walk as far away as we can. That way, we can be alone without someone coming to ask you for something. I'm sorry I haven't been around on my off time as much as I should. There is something that I'm checking on and I can't give you details at the present time. Would you trust me until I can share everything, no matter how hard it gets?"

"That's putting a lot of trust in place when I've not known you that long. I know your references were all good and you have proven yourself around here. It really is none of my business what you do on your time off. We have both acknowledged that we feel a strong attraction to one another. I'm sure you can understand why that puts me in a very questionable position," said Sharon.

"I understand what you're saying, but I'm asking you to place a trust in me that I don't deserve," replied Jason.

"All right, I will but if I find you deceptive in anyway, you are gone from here with no questions asked!" exclaimed Sharon.

"That's all I can ask. Now as far as my past relationships are concerned. I have only had one relationship with a woman in my life. I was very much in love. I was twenty-five years old at the time. I had just started out as a Police Rookie, and I had a partner. We were real buddies and always looked out for each other, or so I thought.

However, it turned out that he and my girlfriend were seeing each other behind my back. They fell in love, and they married. It broke my heart, and I swore that I would never let another woman do the same thing to me again. That's all that I have to say in this matter. I have not felt anything like I feel for you, even for that gal."

"I'm sorry that you had such a betrayal Jason. When someone you trust breaks your heart or your confidence, it plays a major hurt in your life. You need to forgive them so that the bitterness doesn't stay in your heart. Have you been able to forgive them?" asked Sharon.

"I have tried, but it comes back to haunt me every time I think of them."

"Sometimes it takes quite a few forgiveness's to take it away," replied Sharon.

"You have made a change in my heart. I want to make certain that what we are feeling for each other is true and will last. You've had a husband and a good marriage."

"You know what it's like to be happy and live for one another. I want that, but I am so concerned that I will never attain or enjoy another woman in my life. If it is to happen, I hope it will be with someone like you Sharon. I don't want to go fast as my heart needs to heal."

"Well, let's be friends and see where that takes us. In the meantime, it is getting late, and morning will be here before we know it. Lots of guests to look after and satisfy." suggested Sharon.

"I'll walk you back to the main house so no boogie men can get you," joked Jason.

They both chuckled, "Thank you, kind sir!"

As they walked together Jason put his arm around Sharon and held her close. Both had a lot to think about before this went any further in their relationship.

Raymond thoroughly enjoyed his time with Janice. "I've enjoyed this evening so much Janice. Getting to know you and being with you has been even more enjoyable than I could imagine."

"For me too Raymond! It was so nice just getting away and leaving everything behind. Thank you so much!"

Raymond walked Janice up to the door holding her hand but he didn't try to kiss her. This was a good start to help her break out of her shell. They could be well on their way to a fine romance. He left her whistling "Some Enchanted Evening!" as he walked to the Boat House.

~~~

Time for another exchange of guests. The spring had been so beautiful with the glittering lake, the cry of the loons in the night, and the superb food.

The guests had been so easy to accommodate, except for Mr. Stafford. There was no satisfying him. He had lost his wife a year ago and had come to The Sanctuary thinking he would enjoy the surroundings. All the staff had catered to him, trying to fill the gap she had left in his heart. It hadn't worked.

~~~

Janice felt bad for Mr. Stafford, "We are so sorry for your loss. It's hard when you have had a good mate and marriage to be on your own. But I want to tell you that there is hope. My partner, Sharon, has been a widow for five years. Her husband was a fireman. He was out jogging and noticed smoke and fire coming out of a house.

He put a call through to 911 but went inside to check it out. He found a young boy and was carrying him out when there was an explosion. They both died. The parents of the boy had gone to visit next door and thought he would be fine.

Sharon was devastated and it took a lot of prayer to bring her through the mourning period. Look at her now, she is vibrant and content. God can bring you through that too Mr. Stafford. Just have hope and trust the Lord to do it for you!"

"Thank you my dear, I'm sorry I've been such a grump. I need to give it some time. Maybe I'll come back next year and give it another try!"

"That sounds just fine Mr. Stafford. You are always welcome at the Sanctuary," replied Janice.

Things were running quite smoothly at The Sanctuary which gave Jason extra time to do some investigative work. Sharon was a little more tolerant of his times away but still rather apprehensive. He was on his way to town to visit Mathilda Thompson, Lorna's mother.

She had moved in with her sister after her husband Walter died. Jason had high hopes of getting a break in the case after talking with her.

As he drove to the little cottage, he couldn't help noticing the scent of the honeysuckle that came from the lush bushes overflowing with the flowers, giving off such a powerful fragrance.

All the flowers and fresh painted white picket fence were well tended. The white veranda across the front of the house had some comfortable chairs on it. Quite inviting.

It was evident that the sisters enjoyed the house and cared for their property. "Please Lord, let me get something here that will give us a lead."

"Good morning, Mrs. Thompson, I'm Jason Morris, thank you so much for seeing me."

As I mentioned on the phone, we are looking to the whereabouts of your adopted daughter Lorna. Do you have anything of hers that would have DNA on it? A brush or some clothing? Has she been in touch with you since she left?" asked Jason.

"No, she hightailed it out of here when she was sixteen and never looked back. I can't say as if I blamed her. I know my husband was not good to her and some of the things she told me, I just couldn't believe he could possibly do to her. I have kept a little brush and comb, and her first cutlery set from when she first came to us at one-year-old. She was such a cute little thing. Her parents had died, and she had no relatives that would take her in. So, we took her in and fostered her at first then adopted her. I can get her little brush and comb and the little fork and spoon that she just loved, if that would help any. I don't know if they'll do any good, but you can have them. She was a sweet little thing but changed as she grew up. She became very withdrawn and kept to herself."

"You have no idea how much good these will do to help us Mrs. Thompson. Thank you so much. If Lorna does try to contact you, please give me a ring ok. Here is my business card," replied Jason.

As Jason left with the bagged items, he now had high hopes of tying her to these murders. Working it out in his mind, he thought, 'This was the only thing that made any sense at all. The order of their deaths fit the drawing of the straws. But the poison, what kind of poison did she use? I need to investigate the poison more closely as well. How did she drug them to kill them?'

'Yes, I'll send the brush and comb off immediately to forensics with a rush on it. There are hairs on the brush which should make all the difference and give us a good DNA reading. We only have a short time left before July 1st. We are going to have to put around the clock protection on Paul Ashton soon. Lord, we need a break in this case.'

Dinner was almost ready when Raymond heard a loud crash coming from the Dining Room. He rushed to see Janice sprawled on the floor with broken glass all around her. She had been cleaning the windows and the ladder fell into the window and she went forward with it. She was bleeding but more embarrassed than hurt. She had a huge cut on her left arm and scrapes on her face. She was able to get up, but she would need stitches in that arm.

"I don't know what happened to that ladder. It seemed steady enough. What a mess."

Sharon had come running when she heard the crash.

"I will have to drive you into the hospital to get stitches in that arm. Honestly Janice, when will you ever learn? Raymond, would you get a wet towel to wrap around her arm."

"Martha, please clean up this glass and call Jason to come and fix this window and Toni you'll have to help serve the dinner. We will be back as soon as we can."

～～～

As they drove off Sharon was annoyed "Janice, why are you always overextending yourself? Why do you think we have Jason around? He is the one who is supposed to clean the windows."

"I'm sorry Sharon, he is just so busy, and I didn't think there would be any problem. I still don't know what happened to the ladder. It just slipped. At least I won't have to have another Tetanus Shot. You know how I hate needles."

They arrived at Dr. Phillips' office where the nurse took them right in. She shook her head as she remembered Janice coming in just a short while ago. It wasn't so bad after all. Doctor Phillips said, "This certainly could have been a lot worse. You must have had a guardian angel looking out for you Janice."

"I would hate to see your angel at the end of each day. Probably covered in scratches and bruises. Probably worn out as well, wouldn't you think!" he joked.

～～～

In the meantime, everyone back at The Sanctuary worked together and got everything cleaned up and the meal served.

Jason made a quick trip to purchase the glass before the Hardware store closed. He was able to put the new window in right away, so everything was back to normal by the time Sharon and Janice got back from the doctor's office.

Janice was going to have a sore arm for a few days and lots of aches and pains from that fall, but she would be fine. Sharon was grateful that it hadn't been any worse.

"Janice, please promise me you'll let Jason do the windows and heavier work from now on," suggested Sharon.

"You just look after the little fix me ups. Okay? That will save my nerves for sure!"

~~~~~

"I'll promise not to take on anything that I can't handle," replied Janice. with tongue in cheek. She knew she would have trouble keeping that promise as she liked tinkering and making things right.

Back at The Sanctuary the guests were getting ready for bed. It seemed as if the episode in the Dining Room had caused a little unrest in the guests, and they were talking among themselves.

Jason overheard them and came in "Now folks, don't be worried, Janice will be fine. You must have a little excitement in your time here, so you'll be able to go back home with a story of how the Lady of the House fell through the window. It was a miracle that she only had the cut on her arm with a few scratches to her face. You can even say there were angels catching her."

Now don't you think that will give your friends even more of an incentive to visit here where the angels are visiting?" The guests laughed and went off to bed in a much better frame of mind.

When Sharon and Janice arrived back, Jason and Raymond greeted them. Raymond went right around to Janice's side of the car and helped her out. She stumbled as she got out of the car and Raymond was right there to catch her. She looked embarrassed once again.

"You must think I am the clumsiest person alive. You always seem to be catching me in some predicament. Really, I am not that clumsy." Janice explained.

"That's all right just as long as I'm around to catch you." smiled Raymond. They walked up to the veranda together.

Jason and Sharon came together in front of the car. "Is she alright? That was a nasty fall. I believe she has a guardian angel besides Raymond looking out for her." Asked Jason.

"Yes, I believe she was shaken up quite a bit, but she'll be all right with a good night's rest. She promised me she would stop doing the jobs that are your responsibility. But that remains to be seen! Was everything okay here Jason?" asked Sharon.

"Yes, we all pulled together and served the meal and cleaned up. I was able to get the glass in town before they closed. The guests were a little upset, but I was able to send them to bed laughing. We were all concerned for Janice."

―――

"Thank the Lord, it was not as bad as it could have been. Jason, thank you so much for being here to fix the window and bring humor in our midst. You have no idea how it makes me feel. You are a steady hand at the stern, and you make me feel very protected. Thank you so much!"

With that Jason gave her a little kiss on the check and a quick hug and walked her up to the veranda where they said good night. Sharon was feeling the tenderness of Jason's care and began to think it was something she could get used to very easily.

―――

Jason had learned that Lorna Thompson was building her muscles up at the gym and when she worked at the nursery and was now looking quite masculine. She had cut her hair very short and wore clothing that was not very flattering for a woman. Was she preparing to carry out her last revenge on Paul Ashton? Time will tell.

―――

So far, she was the only one that could be linked to these murders. She had a strong motive but how had she got close enough to poison them, then string them up on a stake like a human scarecrow? She may have gotten stronger with her workouts but surely, she wasn't that strong, or was she? Jason wondered.

In each murder, the farmer had been on his own. The first one drank more than his share of alcohol and when autopsied had a high level of alcohol in his system. His wife had left him because he often lost his temper and hit her in his drunken rages. She had had enough and left him to find a safer environment with their two boys.

The second one was on his own as his wife was a nurse at a nearby town and had stayed overnight because she was tired after her long shift. He was alone when the murder took place.

―――――

The third was a bachelor and only had hired hands that came in during the day and left for their own homes after their shifts.

If Lorna was the murderer, how did she do it all by herself. Maybe she had an accomplice help her. Time was running out. They were either going to have to catch the murderer before the July 1st anniversary or watch Ashton's farm very carefully day and night until after July 1st.

―――――

Raymond felt that he was making a little headway with Janice but getting past that shyness was certainly not easy. She was always busy around the property, and he was busy in the kitchen preparing the meals. He was going to have to think of a strategy to reel her in. He'll ask Sharon for a hint or two to help him.

As Sharon came into the kitchen, Raymond asked, "Sharon, can you give me any insight into how I can get closer to Janice."

"I feel a strong attraction to her, and I am sure she is feeling something as well toward me. Has she said anything to you about me or her feelings about me?" asked Raymond.

Sharon had a huge grin on her face. "I'm certain she is feeling something she has never experienced before, and I believe it's a little frightening for her. I suggest you just keep talking to her when she helps you in the kitchen. Keep drawing her out. I am sure she will melt down as she begins to feel safe with you."

Raymond started preparing the meat, "I've never been a patient man. I guess God is trying to teach me to have a little patience. Thanks though, you have given me some hope and I will pray for guidance in 'courting' her."

Sharon left the kitchen with a little chuckle and thought about Janice and Raymond. They certainly do suit each other. Maybe I will put a little bug in her ear to encourage him more.

I know she likes him, and I believe it could turn into something more. Who knows, maybe she will even marry him. Wow, that would be something! She thought.

Janice came around the corner of the house and decided to see if Raymond needed any help in the kitchen. If he only knew how much she liked him.

As she approached the kitchen, she saw Sharon leaving there for the reception area. I wonder what she was doing in the Kitchen. That certainly isn't an area she visits very often. "Hi Raymond, I'm finished with my work and wondered if you needed any help preparing dinner?"

"You came just at the right time. I was going to call Toni to come and peel potatoes. How would you like that job?" asked Raymond.

"I certainly can do that for you Raymond. It will give me a great opportunity to try our electric potato peeler you are always raving about," exclaimed Janice.

Raymond thought this was perfect. God you sure care about our every desire! "I was wondering if you would like to go for a drive after we clean up tonight, Janice?"

"That sounds great, I must say as much as I love this place, it's nice to go and do something else. I love fixing things and I don't mind buying the groceries, but a change is as good as a rest they say. I'll look forward to it and thanks for thinking of me, Raymond."

He smiled, "That isn't hard, you are on my mind most of the time." She looked at him and turned her eyes down. Was that a little flush he saw on her face? Things were looking up. "Thank you, God!"

～～～

After the kitchen was cleaned and made ready for breakfast, Raymond and Janice drove away from The Sanctuary, both feeling tired but looking forward to the drive. They were realizing that even with the shyness their conversation and ease in each other's company was very relaxing. They drove on through the hills and valleys of the north country enjoying the beautiful farms and forests.

Raymond took a breath, "Look at that beautiful sunset. Do you mind if we park on that hill overlooking the lake and watch the sunset?"

"That would be wonderful, just to be able to relax and enjoy the beauty of God's creation." As Raymond parked the car he got out and went around to the passenger side to help Janice out. He took her hand and walked with her to a bench which gave them an exquisite view of the sunset.

~~~

As they sat, he placed his arm around her shoulder. "Do you mind Janice; I think you know that I find you very attractive and you touch areas of my heart that I didn't know existed."

"I have to admit you are touching something deep within me that has me wondering what is happening. You must know, this is all new to me. I didn't have time for romance or relationships in Africa and hardly know what I'm supposed to do."

He leaned over and kissed her very gently on the lips. Even in that precious touch, there was a charge that went right to the bottom of her feet. Janice smiled, "Hmm, I like that very much." He took her in his arms and gave her a deeper kiss because she looked so beautiful.

"Janice, I know I need to go very slowly with you, but you are growing so close to my heart."

"Let's sit here, you in my arms and enjoy the beauty that God has put before us. Look at the magnificent colours in the sky. The pinks and blues and touches of turquoise. He certainly has His paintbrush out tonight." They sat together, the comfort of Raymond's arms bringing a peace to Janice that she had never felt from another person. She had experienced that peace when she was with the Lord or at church but had never felt it from anyone else. She whispered, "Thank you Lord!"

Later on, as Janice prepared for bed, she sat and pondered over the time she spent with Raymond. Oh Lord, what is this I am feeling. It is all so new to me. Can this be love?

Please help me to understand and walk with you in this relationship. She sighed, turned out her light and soon fell asleep with a smile on her face and contentment in her heart.

―――∿∿∿―――

Lorna Thompson drove to the shack in the woods, a mile from the place she grew up. If I can pull this off, I'll have satisfied the deep longing of revenge I have nurtured all these years. This'll be the final payback for the years of suffering I have endured.

This place has always been a place of refuge when I was very young. It still has that comfort for me. As she got her gear out of her car, she thought about the satisfaction of paying off the final farmer in humiliation. I will then be able to go about the rest of my life knowing that I had finished the plan that I had mapped out so many years ago. To see it finished would be a relief.

If they only knew the hatred that built up inside me over the years, then they probably would have been more alert to what I was going to do to them. I hope the humiliation, pain, guilt and shame that I have carried all these years will finally be completely gone.

Once this is accomplished, I can move on and forget what happened that fateful day so many years ago, she thought.

I need to stake out Ashton's farm so that I can figure out the details for the July 1st remembrance. Boy, am I ready. Now to get everything I need to finish the job. I'm glad that I have been able to keep the main items together all these years. It means a lot less gathering for me, she thought.

~~~

Jason was working on one of the rooms that Sharon wanted to get finished. Sharon had designed it down to the minute detail. This room was going to be named The Quiet Place, with forest green walls and sturdy and comfortable oak furniture. He needed Sharon to come and put the final touches on the room with the linens and curtains.

She had chosen white linens, and pastel shades of green and white for the spreads and curtains. He thought, she certainly knows how to make a room a home. Timing perfect, Sharon entered with her arms full of new linens and bedding.

"Jason, would you please get the curtain rods and install them while I make the beds and get the curtains ready for hanging?"

"You batcha!", he said as he walked by her and gave her a little peck on the cheek. She gasped and gave him a look, but inside she was pleased. She just didn't want him to know how much. As she made the beds, she thought about him and wanted to be able to trust him more, but she still wondered about where he went, and lately it seemed like he was away every time he was off duty.

I sure would like to know what he's doing but since he asked me to trust him, please Lord, help me to do just that. If this isn't right, then please show me. She prayed.

Jason came back and put the curtain rods up and hung the curtains as Sharon directed in every exact place where they needed straightening. The room was beginning to take shape. All she needed now was the little finishing touches. She decided she would drive into town and pick up a few treasures at 'April's Unique Gift Shop'. April carried such unique items and Sharon was always able to find just the right item for each room she had been decorating.

As she drove toward town, she saw an old green Chevy truck that was in very bad shape. She noticed a strange man in it. For some reason, he gave her a start. What was it that put her on high alert or set her on edge?

He certainly wasn't a local, but the area was always full of people from out of town, so why the little quickening? Lord, what am I feeling? She prayed.

She drove on pondering the feeling and soon forgot about it as she drove to her favorite store, 'April's Unique Gift Shop'. Now she would pick up those special items that would finish the room. She was so excited as she loved decorating. Now they would have another room to use for guests. Sharon still had two more rooms to decorate before she was finished with the decorating of every available room at The Sanctuary.

She would have to make sure that their renovations were not disturbing the guests. So far no one had complained, and these three rooms were at the back of the house away from the present guest rooms. The noise was minimal.

As soon as Jason finished the chores, he drove off to Paul Ashton's farm. It was only a few weeks until July 1st. The sheriff had one of his deputy's keeping an eye on the place. So far nothing was unusual. Jason was trying to keep his mind on business, but Sharon was on his mind much more than he liked.

He was here to do a job and this job was important as he felt that it was to be his last. He wanted to retire and settle down. He kept thinking that it would be the desire of his heart to settle down right here with a very charming lady. Lord, if this is your will, let it work out that both of us will want the same outcome. I'll share my background with her but it will have to wait until this case is solved.

Paul Ashton tried to go about business as usual, but the murders of his friends were always in the back of his mind. Lately, the memories had been coming more to the forefront.

He was very anxious and hoped that Jason and his team would get to the bottom of everything before July 1st rolled around. He was having nightmares, and his sleep was not peaceful. There was a great fear that he had never known before.

Paul saw Jason drive up and went over to the car. "Have you any more information on the killer?" Jason shook his head. "No!"

"We are tracking the DNA sample from her adoptive mother, and so far, haven't any evidence from the crime scenes that has any DNA on them. I know this must be a terrible time for you. We are doing our best. Have you seen anything unusual around the area? Have you seen anything suspicious?" asked Jason.

"No, I haven't, but then I have been busy with the animals and the other work around the farm."

"As soon as I have anything, I will let you know. In the meantime, make certain you let us know if you see any vehicles that look like they might be watching your place. Let us know immediately."

With that final word Jason drove off. He knew how worried Paul Ashton was and certainly couldn't blame him. His life was definitely in danger. The error of his ways as a young man has come back to haunt him in a way that many would believe as a nightmare and justice for a wrong done!

This evening Jason decided to ask Sharon to go for a drive with him. He didn't have much free time to himself and wanted to spend it with her when possible. He prayed that she would be open to it and that they would be able to share their hearts with one another. He would ask her as soon as he got back to The Sanctuary.

As he drove some distance, he noticed an old green beat up truck on the road. This was definitely one he had not seen before. He took the license number so he could check it with the authorities. No sense taking chances with the July 1st deadline drawing so near.

When he arrived at The Sanctuary there seemed to be some disturbance coming from the kitchen. He ran up to the house and into the kitchen to see that there had been a small fire on the stove. Smoke was going up the exhaust fan and filling the kitchen.

"Raymond, what on earth?"

"It was stupid of me. I turned away and forgot that I had hot oil in a pot. Of course, it caught on fire. Thank God for baking soda. I always keep it close to the stove as it makes a good extinguisher.

We just need to get the smoke out of here then it will be all right."

"What were you thinking?" asked Jason, "You know better than to leave oil on a burner." Raymond grimaced.

"Janice has been on my mind so much that I literally forgot I had turned it on. I need to get a handle on this relationship. It's driving me crazy."

"Well, my dear brother, you had better do something before you burn the place down." Joked Jason.

"Yeah, I know what you mean, these two ladies are diamonds, and we need to look at every facet of their personalities."

Jason grinned "I'm going to ask Sharon to go for a drive with me tonight. Why don't we make it a foursome and drive into town to the cafe?"

"That would be a great idea! It'll give me something to look forward to rather than spending the evening looking at you!"

"Yes, you are moping around like a lovesick puppy, it gets rather boring. I'll go and ask them if they can afford the time," suggested Jason.

Jason approached the reception area and saw that Sharon and Janice were in a deep discussion. He wondered whether he should approach them at all. However, they looked up and saw him and smiled as he drew near.

———〜———

"Raymond and I were wondering if you two ladies were free to take a drive into town tonight after everything is cleaned up?"

Sharon and Janice looked at one another and you could tell from both their expressions that they thought it would be a great idea. They both nodded a yes!

"Well then as soon as we're all finished the chores, Raymond and I will be waiting at my car to drive you both into town. We can stop at Joe's Cafe and have some dessert and coffee and then take a drive along the lake. It's a beautiful night."

The ladies nodded their heads in agreement. The smiles were very evident, and it was obvious that they would look forward to their time with the two brothers.

Janice whispered, "I hope the time until then goes quickly. I have been wanting to spend more time with Raymond and we're always so busy. I'm going to ask Toni to stick around tonight to look after any requests from the guests."

~~~

As the four drove into town, there was an air of anticipation in the car and Raymond sat very close to Janice. Very softly he said, "Would you mind if I put my arm around you? It has been so long since we have had any time together."

Shyly Janice nodded her okay and snuggled into the crook of his arm and looked at those beautiful warm blue eyes which gave her stomach the warm fuzzy feelings once again. There certainly was an electricity between the two of them which both were aware of and didn't seem to mind.

Jason and Sharon were sharing about their day as they drove along. Jason had some problems with the boat but was able to get the engine purring perfectly. He couldn't speak about the case and wished that he could share more with Sharon. It would be nice to talk things over with her. She has so much wisdom and a discerning heart, Jason thought.

Sharon was able to sense a closeness with Jason that was developing more and more as they spent time together. She was wondering what it would be like to kiss him and was hoping that maybe tonight they would be able to spend some time, just the two of them.

It was nice having Raymond and Janice along as the two brothers got along so well. It appeared as if they honored each other, and both had a love for the Lord that made Sharon and Janice very happy.

Jason drove up to Joe's Café and as the four entered in, Joe's wife Tori, was the first to greet them. "Well, what do we have here? Are there budding romances starting with you four?"

Raymond spoke up, "We were all hungering for that delicious Dutch Apple Pie you are so famous for. Also heard Joe has a new cappuccino machine which we thought would be great to try?"

Tori looked suspiciously at them but went along with the explanation. You couldn't fool her. She could sniff out gossip and romance better than any high paid detective. You could feel the magnetism in the four. Now let's see, which two go together best? We'll just have to watch and see! Tori thought.

They enjoyed their time together in the cafe testing the cappuccinos from Joe's new machine.

The homemade Dutch Apple Pie a la mode hit the spot and they left laughing about Raymond's baking and comparing them with Tori's creations.

Jason drove toward the hills so they could watch the sunset and take walks together as couples. He was wanting to hold Sharon close and if the opportunity came was hoping for an embrace and the possibility of a kiss. It was too long coming!

The two couples separated as they got out of the car, Jason and Sharon went immediately down to the beach and Raymond and Janice took a seat on their special bench.

Jason and Sharon walked along, and he took her hand. She didn't pull it away for which he was very thankful.

He felt the relationship had been progressing even though they didn't get much time alone. Just the passing by or working together each day was bringing them closer. Once they were well down the beach, Jason turned to face Sharon and pulled her into his arms.

She drew close willingly, and looked into the depths of those dark brown eyes that were so warm and the longing she felt in her heart stirred between them. As she looked up at Jason, he touched her lips with his fingers, "Sharon, you are so beautiful, and I love the way you just seem to fit in my arms."

She sighed and looked at him expectantly. It was then that he tipped her head toward him and kissed her gently on the lips.

The spark ignited between them, and he kissed her again, only this time she felt it to the very bottom of her feet. The longing in both their hearts became a fervent desire on their lips.

Sharon spoke ever so softly, "I feel so close to you. I never thought that I would feel this way with anyone again. Bill left such a hole in my heart and life. One that I felt would never be filled again, but you have filled that hole to overflowing and I'm so thankful to God that He brought you here to me!"

Jason smiled, "You have brought me to life, and I want to spend more and more of my time with you. I feel that the Lord has something very special for you and me and I believe he has great things for The Sanctuary. I want to be able to share those great things with you. I know it seems like we're moving very quickly, but there is a life to live, and we need to live it to the fullest."

They stood there locked in each other's arms watching the sun go down. Sharon had not felt such contentment in her heart for many years. Thank you, God, I am so thankful for a chance at love once again. I have missed having a man's arms around me.

The Lord had got his paintbrush out once again. You could not imagine a more beautiful sky. The pastel shades of blue, pink, orange and yellow were all strung out like a painting. No artist could capture the magnificent beauty on canvass. Only God could create something so beautiful.

~~~

Raymond and Janice talked about their feelings and the feelings of Jason and Sharon. "Do you think they will allow the Lord to show them how much they are meant for each other?"

Janice sighed "It has taken Sharon a long time to get over Bill's death, but I think she has seen a goodness in Jason that has touched her deeply. Obviously, there is an attraction between them. I thank God that He brought the two of you here. You have been everything we needed and then some!"

Raymond took Janice in his arms and kissed her "This is the beginning of a beautiful relationship that I believe has been ordained by God! I believe He has been saving both of us for such a time as this!"

Janice held Raymond tightly, "You have no idea how long I've waited for you. I know that we were meant for each other. I will never stop thanking the Lord for allowing me to know and love you. You are my Prince Charming and the soul mate that I have been waiting for all my life!" exclaimed Janice.

Once again, they embraced and enjoyed watching the setting of the sun. The masterpiece painted by their Lord and Savior. As they drove back to the property, there was a new sense of belonging among all of them. It was as if something had come out into the open and was now blossoming like a fresh flower in Spring.

~~~

The following morning was so beautiful Sharon decided to take an early walk down to the dock.

She stood by the railing watching three Monarch butterflies flying and playing together. Then one of them came and landed on her foot, wings spread out like an eagle. She dared not move as she was so touched that it had felt safe enough to land on her. It stayed there for some time, its feelers tickling her toes and then moved up her sandal and turned looking outward with wings raised.

After sitting there for a minute or so, it took off. Lord, how beautiful! We are to be a safe resting place and that is what we want The Sanctuary to be for everyone that comes here! Thank you for the reminder!

~~~

Lorna Thompson was noticing a lot of action around Paul Ashton's farm. This was going to complicate her usual format for the revenge. What is going on there? Even the Sheriff's car was there one day.

Was she going to have to rethink her usual plan. She had waited too long to complete this revenge. Nothing was going to stop her on this final vendetta. She could not let this go.

Only her freedom from the past would begin when she completed this revenge. These four men ruined every day of her life. The only desire in her life was for each one of them to die. She had never been able to take revenge on her adoptive father, but she knew when he died it was time to put her plan into action.

Jason had heard back from the team that the green pick-up was registered to a Lionel Torrence. They were researching the address as there seemed to be some discrepancies in the information on file. He put a rush on it and told them to get it straightened out and to give him the results as soon as possible. The deadline was only a week away and they were no closer to finding Lorna Thompson.

Sharon had been pushing for Jason to start work on another room.

She had decided to call it The Hope Room and could see it all done in soft hues of yellow and brown. As she came out of the office, she saw Janice and asked, "Have you seen Jason this morning, I want to get started on the next guest room?"

"I saw him out by the dock earlier but haven't seen him recently," replied Janice.

As Sharon turned to walk that way, Jason appeared with a smile on his face and held out a beautiful red rose from the garden. "For you my sweet lady!"

"You know how to get to me Jason. Thank you!" She smiled shyly "I was just going to look for you. Do you have time to start on the next guest room?"

"Let's go and look at it now. I must run into town for some supplies, and we can see what I need to start in that room."

It has a beautiful view of the lake and will make another restful spot for some weary or worn-out traveler," suggested Jason.

After checking out the room to see what he needed, Jason drove into town he saw the green truck again and decided to follow it. The man drove into the Cafe and Jason decided to go in as well.

He noticed the man was quite nervous and looked around a lot as if he thought someone was watching him. Jason began a conversation with Joe, the Cafe owner, still watching the man. When the man left, Jason walked over to the table and casually picked up the cup he had been drinking from. He walked out with it and took it immediately to the Sheriff's office. They sent it for forensics to get the DNA with an urgent rush on it.

If this Lionel Torrence was somehow Lorna Thompson, they would have the link they needed. Now all they had to do was catch her in the act.

Within three days, they had their answer. Lionel Torrence and Lorna Thompson were one and the same person. They would have to come up with a plan for July 1st to catch her before she was able to murder Paul Ashton.

"Why do so many criminals use the same initials when they are changing their identification?"

Shaking his head, Jason said, "It's probably easier to remember their initials than completely changing their name and initials. I don't know if there is a psychological reason. I should check that out some time when I have nothing else to do!"

Lorna Thompson had everything ready for her final revenge. Only two more days and then she would be free! She would have to be on her guard because of the activity around the farm but she felt confident that she could do this without getting caught. After all, it had worked all the other times, why not now?

The binoculars allowed her to see without getting too close to the farm. I think I will carry that gun I bought just in case something goes wrong and I must change my tactics. There was a lot of activity, and I will have to time this just right. I must make this work, or I will not be able to go on with my life. It has been too long. I must have my satisfaction. Thought Lorna.

Jason had been planning to remove Paul Ashton from the farm early morning on June 30th. He was going to be dressed as Ashton.

He had already asked for July 1st off from the Sanctuary. He felt they would be able to close this case and then he would leave his post and hopefully retire and work full-time at the Sanctuary.

'God, please let us get this wrapped up so that this town can go back to it peaceful existence and the Sheriff can feel a little more secure in his job.' Prayed Jason.

Things were running well at the Sanctuary. Sharon was looking at the books and could see that financially they were making money. All the guests were happy and almost no one complained. In fact, ever since they opened on April 15th, they had been full and had to turn some bookings down. Sharon needed to get Jason to work with her to finish these last two rooms.

This is fantastic, we are not doing a lot of advertising, all the business is coming from guests telling their friends.

"Thank you, God, we have been so blessed!" " and saying that last prayer out loud.

Janice heard it and said, "I agree, we have been provided for, blessed as no one else could bless us."

"Sharon, have you decided how you want to decorate the last two rooms? I was also wondering if we could do something with the reception area?"

Well, let me get the bedrooms out of the way and then we can look at the reception area. I think I have names for them. I like Grace for one and Joy for the other. What do you think?"

"Sounds okay to me, have you thought of how you want to decorate them?"

"I think the Grace Room will be in ivory with walnut ash floors. The Joy Room will have to be bright; I think splashes of bright yellow. I am still thinking about it," Then Sharon sighed and was gone off in a dream world.

Janice left her knowing she would not hear anything she said for a while as she walked away she thought about Raymond wondering if he needed any help.

Raymond was trying out some new recipes which were a little more time consuming so when Janice came and offered her help, he was delighted. "You came along just at the right time, I'm a little behind trying out some new recipes to tantalize the taste buds of our guests."

"Good, what can I do?" It was fun working together and she wished she could spend more time in the kitchen with Raymond, but her own schedule was pretty heavy.

She loved it when she could fit in some time to not only help him but to spend quality time with him. If they could just become engaged and then marry, then they could have all their evenings together. Her face went red just thinking about the possibility.

Raymond was thinking along those same lines and was beginning to plan his approach. He had even considered buying her a ring. He was feeling that their relationship had developed to the place where she was ready to accept his proposal.

～～～

Jason was busy planning the strategy for the July 1st set-up with the Sheriff. They had decided to remove Paul Ashton from the farm. Since Jason was somewhat the same build and coloring, he would dress up like farmer Paul. Then he could be prepared for the murderer if she should appear on July 1st.

They were pretty sure she had been making her plans. The problem was that they had not been able to find out where she was hiding. Whenever they followed the truck, she never led them to where she was staying. They felt that was the one area that had not been watched as closely as it should have.

Lack of personnel had been a shortfall since the beginning of this investigation. Budgets were always getting in the way, of efficiency and it had better not stop them from closing in on the killer this time.

Too much time and preparation had gone into the planning, and they were counting on it to work. Jason could hardly wait to share more of his life with Sharon.

～～～

The time to retire was now and he had a whole new plan for the rest of his life.

It included one very beautiful and warm woman that always touched the very core of his being when he was around her or always thinking fondly about her.

The guests at The Sanctuary were getting ready to leave on Saturday. The weather had been beautiful, accommodations could not be better, and the food was beyond comparison.

Mrs. Warren smiled "Sharon, you have a little bit of Heaven here and I can't wait to come back next year!"

Sharon gave her the receipt "Mrs. Warren, it has been such a pleasure to have you. We have found that all our guests have been so easy to please. We'll look forward to seeing you next June."

Finally, all the guests were gone and Sharon, Janice and the staff took a little break together to share any ideas or problems they had during the past week. They would learn from their mistakes and each week make it even better than the last one, until they reached perfection.

Raymond had whipped up a nice assortment of cold cuts, veggies, and some delicious breads. He had even saved some of his special butter tarts, for Sharon, because he knows how much she loves them. was in a wonderful place, and they decided to pray and thank the Lord for such wonderful guests and to ask the Lord to keep all the staff safe.

If Sharon had any idea of what was ahead for Jason, she would have been lifting up some pretty specific prayers for him. After the break they all went back to their duties preparing for the next batch of guests coming Sunday afternoon.

~~~~~

July 1st had finally arrived, and Jason and the Sheriff's staff were all ready and in place for whatever Lorna Thompson had planned for Paul Ashton. Farmer Ashton had been removed and Jason was ready to do his part as a stand in for him. He was as ready as he could be with a bullet proof vest and a gun in his side pocket. He prayed "Lord, please let us have the wisdom to handle this situation in a way that no one gets hurt."

Lorna Thompson had all her supplies set up at the edge of the farm. It was 4:00 a.m. and she would get the huge tub with the poison insecticide in it close to the barn.

She had felt to bring the gun as she was very nervous about this last part of her revenge plan. It was tucked safely in her belt for quick action. She was not going to take any chances. If she had to shoot him, then that is what she would do. This just had to work!

~~~~~

I don't know why I think this should be any different. The tub on the wagon moved along to the barnyard without any problem. She had the mask ready so the fumes would not touch her once she lit the poison insecticide, and the whistle to get his attention. The moon was full and gave a good light so that it was easier for her to see. As she prepared to light the poison insecticide, she heard steps on the gravel behind her.

"You are under arrest, do not move." She grabbed her gun and spun around and shot as quickly as she could. Jason fell to the ground in a bundle, and then there was a lot of yelling. The Sheriff and his men came running toward her with guns drawn, and to Jason who lay in a heap on the ground. Before they could get to her, she turned the gun on herself and went down with a thud. The Sheriff immediately called 911 for an ambulance as Jason had been shot and was bleeding heavily. They didn't want him to bleed out.

They saw that Lorna had shot herself in the head. If only they were able to get to her quicker. She was not able to complete her revenge and Paul Ashton had escaped with his life. The Sheriff hoped Jason could say the same thing as the ambulance arrived.

The ambulance arrived and took Jason to the hospital where he was going the have to fight for his life. All his plans for a life with Sharon at The Sanctuary were hanging in the balance.

The Sheriff told his men to mark the crime scene and collect all the evidence. He was going to go to The Sanctuary and let Raymond know what had happened to Jason.

It was now early evening, and Raymond was in the kitchen cleaning up after the evening meal. When he opened the door to see the Sheriff standing there, he turned white.

"Jason has been shot, an ambulance took him to the hospital. It's pretty bad," replied the Sheriff.

Raymond said "I'll go and tell the ladies and then go to the hospital."

Sharon and Janice had heard the car come in and saw that it was the Sheriff, so they too were already at the door when Raymond approached. "Jason has been shot and is in the hospital. It looks bad!"

Sharon almost fainted "Are you going to the hospital? I want to come with you."

Janice said, "I'll stay here and instruct Martha and Toni.

Raymond and Sharon arrived at the hospital to find that Jason was already in surgery and would be there for a couple of hours. They had to wait until after the surgery when the doctor would come in to let them know how bad it was. "What on earth was he doing to get shot?" Sharon had no idea.

"Sharon, Jason is a CIA agent, and this was to be Jason's last case. He was brought in to investigate the scarecrow murders that have taken place here over the past three years. He was planning on retiring after this case and I know he wanted to share it all with you after this case was closed."

"Let's pray Raymond. 'Father, you know how I feel about this man, and I ask that you do not take another man from my life. I don't think I could handle it. We commit him to your care and thank you that you have his best interests and mine too at heart. We ask this in the name of your son, Jesus Christ. Amen'"

~~~~

After some time, Janice came into the surgery waiting room and asked Sharon and Raymond, "Have you heard anything yet?"

"No, we have been waiting for some report from the Doctor, but no one has come from the Operating Room yet."

"Can I get you some coffee or something? You must be hungry," asked Janice.

Both Raymond and Sharon shook their heads "I couldn't eat anything, I would probably throw it up, my stomach is so full of knots," Sharon sighed.

After another couple of hours, the doctor finally came in and smiled. "Well, he gave us a pretty bad scare, but we were able to patch him up. The bullet just missed a main artery, or it would have been a different story."

"It will take a little while for him to recuperate but he will be as good as new before long. He is still in recovery. Once they wheel him into his room, you can go in and see him for a few moments."

They all let out a sigh of relieve "Thank you Lord for your goodness and your mercy!"

As soon as Jason was back in his room, Sharon and Raymond went in. He looked so pale hooked up to the machines. Sharon cried and spoke a prayer out loud, "Oh, God give us the strength to get through this time and let him be completely healed. I can't think how close we came to losing him. Thank you, Lord."

Raymond sighed, "I am so glad that this is his last case. It's time he had some fun out of life instead of working and living only to catch the bad guys!"

Sharon took Jason's hand and leaned over and kissed his cheek. He blinked but did not wake up.

"Raymond, I would like to stay here with him. Do you think you could drive Janice back home and she can leave her car with me?

I'll stay until he wakes up and I will call you to let you know how he is doing. Is that ok with you?"

"Of course!" replied Raymond.

Raymond and Janice left with Raymond holding her close. "Why didn't he let us in on what he was doing? We were so suspicious of his leaving all the time. If we had known, we could have prayed more for him!"

"He could not expose his cover. It was not known whether the murderer lived in the area. He was concerned for the safety of you and Sharon as well as the guests. That is why he asked Sharon to trust him."

It was the next day before Jason showed any sign of waking. Sharon never left his side during the whole time. When he finally opened his eyes, she was right there and he gave her a very weak smile, "I'm sorry!"

She said, "Shh...don't try to speak, just rest and get well. There will be lots of time for that later. In the meantime, just let me hold your hand and pray for you. You gave us all a fright. Raymond and Janice have gone back to The Sanctuary to look after the guests. and I need to let them know that you are awake. I love you Jason, And I never want to be without you ever again, do you hear me?" Once again, he smiled weakly and gave her hand a squeeze. He went right back to sleep, but she knew that he was going to be all right.

The Sheriff and crew cleaned up the mess at the Ashton farm.

They found all the equipment Lorna had ready at the edge of the farm. She certainly knew what she was doing and was ready to hang up another victim. The ingenuity she had in the planning and executing the revenge was remarkable.

Farmer Ashton was so relieved that they had caught her and that now he could move on with his life, without any fear hanging over him all the time. He realized the crime from his younger years could have had a much different ending. He figured it was time for him to make things right with God. He couldn't undo what he did, but he certainly could repent and receive forgiveness even though he did not deserve it.

It had now been several weeks since July 1st and Jason was resting comfortable in the Boathouse. He was getting better but would still not be able to return to work for some time. Sharon had got in touch with her son Daniel, and he was able to come and help out while Jason was healing and recuperating.

It was good to have him around. Daniel was also getting to know Jason and approved of the relationship that was growing between him and his mother. "How much longer before Jason can return to work Mom?"

"The doctor says he should be able to start doing some light work in another month or so. I appreciate you so much and all that you have been able to do to help us out. I don't know what we would have done without you. I wouldn't have wanted to hire a stranger for the short haul. You have done a great job, and you make me proud!"

"I'm so glad that I have capable staff to run the agency, otherwise I would not have been able to do this for you! God has been faithful in this whole situation. He must really love you guys!" Sharon smiled and hugged him "Yes, I'm sure He loves us all."

"I always say that He loves my friends and family, but don't forget that I'm His favorite!" Sharon said in jest.

"Oh, mom!" exclaimed Daniel.

In September Raymond and Janice announced their engagement and were planning a Christmas Wedding. For Janice, it couldn't happen soon enough. She was so in love with Raymond and wanted to spend her life making him happy. Of course, the feelings were mutual, and he was so looking forward to sharing his life with Janice.

"Janice, my love, could you help me in the kitchen?" She came into the kitchen and Raymond caught her in his arms and gave her a kiss that she felt right down to the bottom of her toes.

"This is the help I needed" replied Raymond. "You are a character Raymond," laughed Janice, "I love you and needed that as much as you did!"

The guests were coming and going, and it seemed as if they had been doing this for years rather than just six months. The rooms were all finished thanks to Daniel's skills and Janice's little extras.

It looked like they were going to have a full house for the Christmas season. With the planning of the wedding, it was going to be full scale with all hands on deck.

Jason was sitting by the dock getting very impatient to get back to work and carry his share of the load. Sharon came sauntering down to sit with him.

"I know we have talked about my having to keep secret my life as a CIA agent, but I want you to know I will never keep another secret from you for the rest of my life."

"I realized that you could not share what you were doing with me, but I must say it was very stretching for me to trust you through these months. It was like putting my trust in God. I couldn't feel it or touch it I just had to do it. My trusting Him has helped me to put my trust in you Jason."

"Sharon, I have been waiting to ask you something that I think we both want."

Jason got down on one knee and put his hand in his pocket and brought out a ring box.

"Will you marry me and make me the happiest man in the world?"

"Yes, Jason, I want very much to share the rest of my life with you. You fit into my life and this place like we were made for you! I love you so very, very much!"

~~~

Sharon gasped when she saw the ring, it was the most beautiful pear-shaped diamond with ruby clusters all around it.

"Just one more question my dear. Would you consider making the Christmas Wedding a double ceremony with my brother and Janice?"

"That would be awesome, but we will have to check with them!"

"It's already done, and they are in complete agreement!"

~~~

EPILOGUE

The parlor was decorated with red and white roses in huge standing white wicker containers. There were touches of white tulle everywhere. Each chair had been covered with a cream-colored tailored skirt. A scarlet rose was attached to the back of each chair. The fragrance of the roses filled the air, and the excitement of the guests was tangible.

~~~~~

All the guests had now assembled and were waiting for the brides to come down the aisle. Everyone of Sharon's family had been able to get the time off and the excitement in the air was thick. So her children and grandchildren were all there to be part of this happy occasion. You could feel the joy of the Lord throughout the whole place.

Jason and Raymond were at the front of the room with Pastor David awaiting the entrance of their beautiful brides. You could see the anticipation on their handsome faces. They were both dressed in grey striped trousers with black formal jackets. Their old-fashioned grey cravats added a touch of nostalgia. Raymond's lapel boutonniere matched Janice's bouquet and Jason's was a single red rose.

Sharon and Janice were ready. "Well Janice, did you ever think this day would come?"

"I have been counting weeks, then days, then minutes and seconds, I'm ready, let's go!"

"Things will be very different after today. You and Raymond will be living together in the Boathouse. Jason and I, in our apartment. Lord, help us all to adjust and be happy and content together!"

First to come down the aisle were Sharon's grandson, Larry and granddaughter, Emma. He was carrying a pillow with the rings while Emma scattered rose petals for the entrance of the brides. Sharon's daughters, Mary, the matron of honor and Darlene, the bridesmaid came down the aisle in beautiful red velvet dresses. Then came Janice in an ivory satin gown that was embroidered with fine roses made of seed pearls. She carried a bouquet of red and white roses, and her veil covered her face.

Next came Sharon in a cream-colored silk suit that was tucked in at the waist and the long skirt had a slight slit up the back.

She wore miniature red roses in her upswept hair and carried one single red rose. The rose was in remembrance of the first one Jason had given her this past summer.

As they came down the aisle, all faces looked to them with huge smiles. The two brothers at the front came forward to claim his bride as she came forward. As there were two brides, they had agreed to the old Jewish custom of making sure each groom was getting the right bride. Raymond lifted the veil and put it back from Janice's face claiming his bride. Jason then came and claimed Sharon's hand to receive his bride. As their eyes met, you could feel the electricity and spark ignite and the whole room felt the magnetism of this couple's love.

There was not a dry eye in The Sanctuary as the four were joined in marriage to start their lives afresh as co-workers and owners of the little touch of Heaven God has gifted to them.

The atmosphere in The Sanctuary was one of peace and joy. There was such an anticipation of all the good things to come. The surprises that God had in store for them would come later.

The End

www.ingramcontent.com/pod-product-compliance
Lightning Source LLC
LaVergne TN
LVHW051954060526
838201LV00059B/3634